Truly your God must be the God of gods and Lord of kings and the revealer of mysteries to have enabled you to reveal this mystery." **~ Daniel 2:47**

Also by Suzanne Brody

Dancing in the White Spaces
(2007, Wasteland Press)

Etz Chayim She: Modern Poems Grown from Ancient Texts
(2015, Wasteland Press)

Mermaid Tears
(2020, Silver Bow Publishing)

Lunch with Rav Dimi
(2021, Silver Bow Publishing)

Unearthed
(2022, Silver Bow Publishing)

Serah's Secrets
(2022, Silver Bow Publishing)

Chrysalis Summer
(2024, Ben Yehudah Press)

BODY ON THE BIMA

Suzanne Brody

720 Sixth Street, Unit #5
New Westminster, BC
V3L 3C5
CANADA

Title: Body on the Bima
Author: Suzanne Brody
Publisher: Silver Bow Publishing
Cover Art: "Entering the Afterlife" by Candice James
Editing: Candice James

www.silverbowpublishing.com
info@silverbowpublishing.com
ISBN: 978-1-77403-362-3 paperback
ISBN: 978-1-77403-363-0 electronic book

Library and Archives Canada Cataloguing in Publication
Title: Body on the Bima / Suzanne Brody. Names: Brody, Suzanne, 1976- author. Identifiers: Canadiana (print) 20250219344 | Canadiana (ebook) 20250220725 | ISBN 9781774033623 (softcover) | ISBN 9781774033630 (Kindle) Subjects: LCGFT: Detective and mystery fiction. | LCGFT: Novels. Classification: LCC PS3602.R64 B63 2025 | DDC 813/.6—dc23

For all my friends and colleagues

who can relate

Table of Contents

Author's Note / 9

Prologue / 11

Chapter 1 Sam's Worst Fear / 15
Chapter 2 A Deadly Discovery / 29
Chapter 3 Stay Calm / 37
Chapter 4 Pivoting / 41
Chapter 5 Emma / 55
Chapter 6 - Sam's Story / 58
Chapter 7 - Boiling Over / 76
Chapter 8 - Time to Go Home / 79
Chapter 9 - Lilith and the Antisemite / 83
Chapter 10 - My Turn Begins / 96
Chapter 11-My Last Interactions with Leonard
/ 106

Chapter 12 - Walk 'n' Talk / 115
Chapter 13 - The Big Fight / 120
Chapter 14 - Ethan's Lesson / 145
Chapter 15 - Another Conversation with Lilith / 150
Chapter 16 - A Friend Indeed / 153
Chapter 17 - Back to Work / 160
Chapter 18 - Fresh Air / 169
Chapter 19 - Kitah Kochavim Reconvenes / 181
Chapter 20 - Back to Normal? / 198
Chapter 21 - Another Call with Lilith / 213
Chapter 22 - Getting to Know Detective Tara
/ 219

Chapter 23 - Girl Talk / 230

Chapter 24 - Board Business / 234
Chapter 25 - We All Need Friends / 249
Chapter 26 - A Dynamic Duo / 244
Chapter 27 - Panic Rising / 277
Chapter 28 - A Breath to Think / 286
Chapter 29 - A Suspect in Sight / 291
Chapter 30 - Operation Confession / 297
Chapter 31 – Denouement / 306

Epilogue / 315

Author's Note

This is a work of fiction. If you know someone with the same name as any of the characters, it's because I tried to pick names that particularly "sound Jewish," not because I'm writing about you, your friend, your relative, or anyone else you know. Similarly, some of the characters' behavior or attitudes may make you think of someone you know, but I can assure you all of the characters and events described are indeed fictional. This work is also not meant to be read as a solution to your problematic synagogue politics (I know you have them, too). Murder is not a solution.

Do not murder.

And, I hope you do enjoy this book.

Prologue

My name is Rabbi Shachar Whyte, and I used to feel Synagogue B'kol Makom (or, as it is often called, SBM) was a safe, friendly congregation. I thought I had hit the jackpot when it came to landing this job. Unlike my best friend from rabbinical school, Rabbi Rachel Rubin, and many other female rabbis I know, I hadn't had my clothes or shoes criticized, and no one, not even the older male congregants, had ever called me sweetie. Rachel always presented these stories as amusing anecdotes, but I know how much sexism and disrespect (whether conscious or unconscious) bothered her. I sometimes wonder if Rachel faced more harassment than I did because she looked like a cute little pixie with gorgeous waves of chestnut hair while I had limpish hair that occasionally resembled tree bark, and there was no way I would ever fit into a dress smaller than a size 10. Unfortunately, my sense of having won the job lottery changed drastically this past October.

Nothing in my rabbinical school training prepared me for this! I spent five years learning important Jewish texts like the Torah (sometimes referred to as the 5 books of Moses, the bible, or the old testament, depending on your religious belief system). We also spent a lot of our time studying commentaries, stories, and explanations of the Torah. I even took a class where we learned some distinguishing characteristics of the prophets, and at least one was focused on the details of Jewish history in different countries. I studied the intricacies of halakha (Jewish Law). I read, discussed, debated, analyzed and absorbed a lot of material.

Rabbinical school wasn't all cerebral, though. When we weren't immersed in 2000-year-old texts, we practiced liturgy and the elements of lifecycle events. We even practiced officiating at funerals by creating ceremonies for long-dead celebrities and for imaginary congregants. We familiarized ourselves with the intricacies of Jewish mourning. But never once did we talk about what to do when you find a dead body in the synagogue building!

I never thought the omission of lessons about what the rabbi is supposed to do when a murder victim was discovered on the Bima* right before Shabbat (Sabbath) services would be an issue!

***(the raised platform at the front of the Synagogue where the prayer leader usually stands)**

Chapter 1
Sam's Worst Fear

Maybe if I had known what was about to happen, and what we were about to find, I would have chosen my words more carefully when I was working with Sam and the rest of Kitah Kochavim this past fall. But, never in my worst nightmares had I expected anything like this to happen. Classes for Kitah Kochavim, the 6th and 7th grade students, were held on Tuesday nights in the chapel. All of the kids and teens in the congregation at Synagogue B'kol Makom (SBM) attend public schools with their peers then come here to the synagogue a few hours a week to learn about Jewish practices and beliefs. We have a wing of the synagogue building with classrooms that are used for the younger grades, but as a recognition that the 6th and 7th graders were on the cusp of being considered adults for Jewish ritual purposes, their class was held in the chapel.

The chapel was the first room you saw when you entered the synagogue, and it was not at all "school-like." The chapel's wood floor, fireplace, and eggshell-colored walls tended to put people immediately at ease. On the mantle above the fireplace, were some beautiful candlesticks and a painting that evoked the feel of Jerusalem at sunset on a Friday night. There was a shadowy white figure standing on the well-worn stones of a wall overlooking a golden dome. The background was composed of a mix of pale pink, peach, baby blue, and a gradient of purple. Beside the fireplace, there were cabinets with glass doors through which could be seen books with gold lettering on the spine, some children's picture books, a bin of dinosaurs, and another bin with something blue and soft-looking just barely visible. It was a room that could have been the living room in someone's house, even though instead of comfortable sofas and armchairs, the room was furnished with maroon folding chairs that were frequently moved around into different configurations for seating. Even though there were four windows to let the light in, the blinds were often kept closed so no one could peer in. Instead, a soft yellow glow illuminated the room. It was a room where I felt at ease, and where I held a number of classes and youth services.

In addition to giving the class a bit of prestige, and a sense of being more mature, there were also practical reasons to hold sessions for Kitah Kochavim in the chapel. The chapel's proximity to the front door made it the best room in the synagogue for me to hold evening classes and other programs for both teens and adults. Since the rise in antisemitism around the country, including both vandalism and violent attacks in or near synagogue buildings, a lot of members of our congregation were worried about safety. Like many other Jewish institutions across the country, our community had applied for grants to upgrade our security. One of the new procedures instituted by the synagogue board, and recommended by the security committee, was to keep all the outside doors locked at all times.

Believe it or not, it took 15 adults three months to institute this simple change in procedure, which did not limit their access to the building at all since both the paid staff (myself, the administrative assistant, the custodian, and at least one of the preschool teachers) and a plethora of volunteer lay leaders (synagogue board members, chairs of various committees, and probably a few others, too) had key fobs that opened the locks electronically to let them into the building. The big difference was our new security measures meant everyone else needed to be let in by someone already inside. Practically, that meant having greeters stationed at the door for any class, worship experience, or other programs we offered. Rather than finding a volunteer to monitor the door and open it for the students in Kitah Kochavim, and other evening classes, they were held in the chapel because it was practically adjacent to a door. That meant if someone was late to class, we could hear them knocking and could open the door without really missing anything happening in class. This made the flow of the class run much more smoothly, even if we found out later our security measures didn't actually protect those who were in danger.

That particular Tuesday evening was much like many other sessions I enjoyed with Kitah Kochavim. I chatted with the tweens as they slowly came into class and settled into the seats I had arranged into a circle. I let them have a few minutes to talk about whatever was foremost on their minds (usually this involved tests, teachers, or other kids in their classes). I knew as soon as I told them what was coming, there would be a lot of moans and excuses, so I wanted them to be as calm and present as possible before I began, and I had found this bit of chaotic conversation for the first few minutes had precisely that effect most days.

Once it looked like everyone had arrived, I quickly got their attention and jumped right into my big announcement. "Kitah Kochavim, your class service will be in three weeks. That means in three weeks, at the end of October, you will be the ones leading the prayers on Friday night."

As expected, this announcement was met with a chorus of moans, grumbles, complaints, and excuses.

"Do we have to?" asked Emma Silverman in her typical whiny voice. She often acted as if being asked to do anything at all was beneath her. Her blond hair was always styled in perfect ringlets and pulled out of her face with a cute hair accessory to match her outfit.

I couldn't believe the way she came to class each week wearing clothes that looked like they cost more than I made in a year, and she was still growing! I tend to favor comfortable clothes, that have decent-sized pockets, and are versatile enough for the many different tasks I perform in a given day. But sometimes, I'll admit, I was a bit jealous of Emma's outfits and how put-together and self-assured she looked.

Before the whine stopped, Isaac Weiss groaned dramatically and declared in a bored-sounding tone, "We did that last year."

Isaac's brown hair was long in the front, and often obscured at least part of his face. He also tended to wear baggy hoodies and sit in a bit of a slouch with his feet stretched in front of him. He always acted as if he were here under duress, but I sensed that was just an act he was putting on in front of his peers since he often had insightful comments to add to class discussions.

"I have something else I need to do that day," added Ethan Kleinman quickly. "I think there's a soccer tournament. That's it. A soccer tournament. Sorry, rabbi. I gotta be there for my team. They need me." The grass stains, shin guards, and odor surrounding him made it clear Ethan had come to class that evening straight from soccer practice, but from the way his words tumbled out, I knew he was just giving me an excuse. I also knew, in the end, Ethan's parents would prioritize this class service over a soccer game.

"I think I'm going to be sick!" Sam Rosenberg muttered under his breath as his face took on a pale, greenish tinge.

"Sam, are you OK?" asked Hannah Berman. She was often overlooked because she could be rather quiet in a group setting, but she really was a sweet, caring girl.

Sam shook his head somewhat violently so Hannah nudged the trashcan closer to him, just in case. To move attention away from Sam and to address the complaints and worries before they could start to pile on top of each other, I spoke up, "Yes, Emma, you all have to do it. Ethan, you're part of the team here, too. You did lead a service last year, Isaac, but this one is going to be different. Just because we have services every week doesn't mean we can't make this one different from any other Shabbat service you've ever been to." There were still some grumbles, but I could see there was glimmer of curiosity in some of their eyes. Of course, they immediately demanded to know how it would be different. Fortunately, I had anticipated this and was ready with an answer.

"We're going to be adding special creative elements. I know you have a lot of questions about what that means, and I can see not all of you are ready to trust me yet, but believe me this will be a good thing. I'm going to ask you hold off judgment until the end of class today. You think you can do that?"

They somewhat grudgingly said yes, which I knew to take as more of a reluctant maybe, so I quickly introduced the first task of the evening. Just in case any of them had forgotten, I reminded them it's true there is a certain sameness to services every week. "We say the same prayers each time. In some congregations, the order of the service is so predictable that everyone knows when the rabbi will announce a page number or when there will be a responsive reading in English" I was glad to get a slight chuckle from some of them. I tried to mix things up a little every once in a while, but there were older congregants that really liked the familiarity and predictability of keeping everything exactly the same. There are different tunes that can be used to sing the prayers, but it seems the same handful just keep getting used over and over. But, even within the fixed liturgy, there can be a lot of room for creativity. I knew their eyes would just glaze over if I said anymore, so instead, I pulled over the whiteboard and got two volunteers to write down what everyone said. I had them draw a line down the middle and label one side as "fixed" and the other as "flexible." After making sure everyone was clear on what was meant by each term, I explained their first task was to figure out what aspects of the service had to stay the same and what they could change and write them down in the appropriate column. Then, seeing that his face was still rather pale, I pulled Sam aside to see if I could help him.

"Sam, you didn't look so good just now. Are you OK?"

"No," he said in a small voice.

"What's wrong, Sam? Does this have something to do with the class service?"

"I can't do it!" he wailed.

"Why not?" I asked, both puzzled and concerned.

"I just can't!" he shouted then mumbled into his lap. "OK?"

"Sam," I coaxed in the same tone I might use on a skittish cat, "This isn't the first time you've helped lead a service with your classmates."

"I just can't."

"What are you trying to avoid, Sam?" I asked gently.

"Last time I ran off and barfed," he mumbled.

"I remember you left early, before dinner. But I thought you were sick with a stomach bug. That's what everyone said."

"That's what mom told everyone. But it wasn't a stomach bug."

"I'm so sorry to hear that, Sam. It's OK to be nervous. A lot of people, both kids and grownups, get nervous when they are standing up in front of other people." Even as I said it, I recognized Sam's reaction was more extreme than just being a bit nervous.

"Forget it," he mumbled so softly I barely caught the next couple of words. "I knew no one would understand. I just know this service is going to be even worse than the last one I led."

I really wanted to give the poor kid a hug, but instead I simply said "So, last year's class service didn't go so well for you. That doesn't mean the same thing will happen this year. It's the same service, and you know it even better now than you did last time."

Sam just shook his head "no" and looked like he might even faint. He mumbled something under his breath that I strained to catch. I think he said "I knew no one would get it.

"The other kids will make fun of me, and my dad will get mad. He'll kill me. I am clearly doomed! I'm gonna die right there in the middle of the service and everyone will laugh," he exclaimed with such despair and defeat in his voice.

"Hey, Sam, it's going to be OK," I said, seeing how miserable he looked.

"Yeah, maybe for you. And some of the other kids. Not for me," he said glumly. "I know you're trying to make it all seem like fun and all, but if I have to be a part of this class service, I just know I'll die on the Bima. And obviously my parents will kill me if I refuse to go!"

"Look, you're right, you could get sick again. You could faint or barf or forget the words. I don't think you will do any of those things, but I'll admit there is a possibility. And you probably won't believe me if I tell you none of that is the end of the world. I know you're worried about your dad's reaction, but we both know he won't actually kill you. All of the adults in your life will still love you and be proud of you for the effort you are putting in. And the kids who are your friends won't laugh or tease you. They'll be worried about whether you are OK or not. As for the rest, what they think or say doesn't really matter."

I couldn't tell from Sam's sigh whether any of what I was saying was helping or getting through to him, but I sure hoped it was. I had spied the clock out of the corner of my eye and knew I should try to move Sam on to doing at least some of what was planned for today's lesson. So, with a faint smile, I assured Sam that in all of my years of doing this, I could confidently say no one has ever died on the Bima in the middle of their class service either here or at any of the congregations where my friends work. I told him, 'the more you practice, the more the words will just pour out of you without you even having to think. So let's rejoin your classmates." If only I had known how those words would come back to haunt me.

When Sam and I rejoined the class, I looked at the lists they had generated. There were only a few minor points I had to correct, so I made sure to let them know how well they had done before introducing the next activity. There were a few grumbles when I said they would have to still incorporate the things listed on the "fixed" list, but, they perked up when I told them they could pick up to three things from the "flexible" side of the list and be as creative as they wanted as long as they stayed respectful and within the spirit of the fact that this was, after all, a Shabbat service for the whole community. I gave them a minute to think about what aspect of the service they might want to work on, before I had them move into groups.

After they divided themselves up into groups, and spread out in the chapel and the hallway, they decided on practicing different tunes, composing alternative readings, and figuring out ways to compare the prayers to candy. You might be wondering about that last one. These kids are always super motivated by treats. I told them if they could come up with reasonable comparisons between any of the prayers and candy, I'd make sure we had that candy at the service.

I brought everyone back together so the groups could share their work with each other. Everyone was in such a good mood and so excited about what they had come up with I decided not to remind them they would each still have to lead some of the actual prayers in the "normal" way. It felt good to hear them all chattering excitedly to each other as they left the building and headed out to their parents' cars.

Chapter 2
A Deadly Discovery

Those three weeks flew by, and before I knew it, it was the day for Kitah Kochavim to stand up on the Bima and lead us all into Shabbat. As the start time for the service grew closer, activity in the building increased. The caterers were busy in the kitchen putting the finishing touches on dinner and the custodian was double-checking the bathrooms and doing his best to get the temperature right. I could hear someone in the sanctuary setting up some flowers, and volunteers were setting the tables. Mina Mushkin, SBM's administrative assistant, had let in the evening's greeters and ushers. It wasn't long before I closed the door to my office and went to greet the 6th and 7th graders and their families, as well as the regular Friday night service attendees.

The first thing I heard, as some of the kids walked in was someone saying, "heart attacks killed more people last year than cancer did."

"Wrong! It's heart disease and stroke that claims more lives than cancer and respiratory diseases," corrected a somewhat prissy sounding female voice that must have belonged to Emma.

"Whatever!" sneered the first voice, who I now saw was Ethan. "Still means lots of people die of heart attacks every day!"

Sam's green face came into view surrounded by a couple of his animated classmates. "I think I'm going to die of fright," he mumbled.

"You really can die of fright, you know," piped up another helpful student. "My mom's a doctor and she said when you get really frightened you get this rush of adrenaline and your heart rate goes up and your pupils get dilated. Then your heart muscles can't relax and you lose consciousness."

Yikes! This was a rather disturbing conversation for them to have right before their class service. If we were sitting around a campfire roasting marshmallows that would be a different story. Before the conversation could go any further and the kids could wind each other up and get more panicked, I pulled them all aside and reassured them while they were correct, these awful things could potentially happen, the likelihood was very low. Instead of scaring one another, I asked them what techniques they all knew for calming down. I managed to phrase the question in such a way it was immediately pounced upon as a challenge. Various breathing techniques, counting, paying attention to your senses, and other helpful techniques were all suggested.

Once anxiety levels were all back down in a more manageable range, at least for everyone who wasn't Sam, I checked to make sure all the students were present and accounted for, and that everyone was wearing appropriate clothing. Sometimes when kids or teens get up to lead services skirts are too short, pants are falling down, or someone has on a potentially offensive t-shirt, or someone is unsteady on high heels. Fortunately, everyone looked fine tonight.

I made sure each student had a copy of the program, a siddur (prayer book), and any supplemental readings or other pieces they had prepared. I then showed them the bags and boxes of candy I had bought as promised. I told the class they could use them as props during the service, and they would all get a chance to eat the candy after the service was over. Once they had the treats in hand, I urged them to take their places on the Bima so the service could begin.

As they got up there, I heard Hannah ask, "Why did someone leave their shoes on the Bima? And with the toes pointing to the ceiling, too?"

"Someone left their shoes on the Bima? That's weird!" echoed Emma.

"Um, guys, I don't think those shoes are empty..." said Ethan.

"What do you mean, not empty?" asked Hannah. "You mean someone is sleeping on the Bima? There are much better places in this building to take a nap!"

Sam didn't say anything, but his face took on a sicklier tone than just moments before. This did not look like his usual nerves.

"OK everyone," I said calmly as I faced the class. "Please take a breath. And could someone tell me what has you all huddled together like this? And why are you talking about shoes and places to nap?"

Without speaking, Sam pointed to the floor in front of him. I couldn't see what he was pointing at because there was a large reader's table (like a triple-wide lectern) separating me from the students. I could hear his teeth start to chatter like he was trying to talk but couldn't get any sounds out.

"Those shoes are definitely not empty," said Ethan with more certainty than before.

"Th-th-there's someone lying on the floor," Emma managed to say. "And... and... and I think that might be blood!" she said with her voice rising higher and shakier with each word.

"Somehow, he seems to have fallen under the reading table," commented Isaac in a voice that sounded unnaturally calm.

"Good point," said Ethan. "Otherwise it might be his head sticking out and his legs hidden behind that cloth thingy."

Hannah pulled Emma into a hug and turned to look at me with wide eyes. "I think he's hurt," she said, adding "no one just takes a nap under the reading table, do they?"

"But, if he's hurt, what do we do?" asked Sam.

"Let me take a look," I said calmly as I walked around to where they were all standing.

Even though my heart was beating faster and faster as the shoes in question came into view, I knew I needed to stay calm and in charge for the sake of the students and everyone else who had come to the service. If I didn't handle this carefully, I could see how something unexpected like this could quickly devolve into one of pure panic with rippling ramifications for student enrollment, synagogue membership; and even my own career future here could be compromised and could affect my chances as to anywhere else I might want to go later.

I lifted the edge of the cloth that covered the reader's table from which the shoes protruded. Not that I had doubted them, but the students were right. Those brown dress shoes were not empty. My eyes traveled up the legs that were covered in creased gray slacks and I took in the sight of someone lying down on the carpet. The light was dim and I didn't want to raise the cloth any higher, but it looked like the carpet around the person was really dirty. I really hoped I was just imagining I saw parts of this person's brain...

I refused to scream. I needed to keep calm for the sake of the kids. I repeated that last thought over and over to myself as if it were a mantra that would magically make this go back to a normal service led by students. The class was the quietest and stillest I had ever seen them as they waited for me to do something. They stared at me expectantly. I may have sounded a little bit unhinged, but I made sure to stay out of range of the microphones as I cleared my throat and asked the class, "do any of you read mysteries or watch crime shows or hospital dramas?" My question was just odd enough their faces slowly took on a look of puzzlement rather than panic or horror. It took only a minute but felt like an hour before a couple of hands started to inch up.

"Excellent," my heartbeat began to gradually slow back down as I watched the change in their expressions and gathered my courage to take charge of the situation.

"So in those books or on those shows, what's the first thing someone is supposed to do if they find a person who seems to be really hurt?"

"Call 911," said Ethan.

"And if they think something about the situation seems suspicious?" I asked.

"Don't touch anything. Call the police," a tentative voice said. "But usually they do end up touching something they shouldn't before they finally get around to calling the police."

"They might not call the police right away, but we will," I said calmly. "And we'll all step away and not touch anything."

I selected one of the students who looked the most collected and asked her to please bring Mina over. Not onto the Bima, I clarified, but close enough that I could speak with her without leaving the class or using the microphone. I didn't need her to see what I strongly suspected was not just an injured person but a 'dead body, possibly a murder victim. The student complied quickly, and I filled Mina in on the basics of the situation.

"Don't panic," I said to Mina, realizing as I said it that it was an awful way to start. "But, we have a situation here."

Mina's eyes went wide. "A situation? What do you need me to do?"

"Call the police, please. Let them know we've found a body."

Chapter 3
Stay Calm

"A body?" Mina's voice trembled and managed to go up an octave.

"Yes," I did my best to whisper and stay away from the microphones. "So I need you to call 911 to report it. And when they arrive, please bring the police over to the Bima here in the Sanctuary as discreetly as you can so no one gets freaked out. The body's on the floor mostly under the reading table. While you do that, I'm going to move everyone into the Chapel. On TV., they always talk about preserving the scene and keeping everyone there so the police can talk to them. I'm going to presume there is some truth to that, and do my best to keep everyone away."

Mina swallowed, and I watched her win the struggle to hold back further questions or reactions for now. She nodded and headed off to call the police while I turned back to the class, still standing in a cluster around me. None of them had moved a single muscle, though I got the impression if they were younger, at least half of them would be hanging on to my skirt. I quietly told them we were all going to the Chapel, and Mina had gone to call the police. Once the police came, we would all follow their instructions. But, for now, they were free to head over to the chapel, as long as they all stayed together. They nodded and began filing off the Bima as I stepped over to the microphone farthest away from the body.

Most of the parents and other adults who had come for the service were oblivious to the drama on the Bima. A group of them were still chatting in the back of the room, while a few others had settled into seats in anticipation of the service. I was surprised at how calm and even authoritative my voice sounded as I said, "Shabbat Shalom" and looked out at the gathered crowd. I was pleased to see not just the families of the students leading the service who had come. Some of the Friday night regulars and a few board members were also in attendance. There was even a new face I didn't recognize. Any other time I would have been delighted to welcome a newcomer to our services. But I was laser-focused on keeping everyone calm and it wasn't until later I began to wonder about this unfamiliar person. My thoughts and emotions swirled in my head while I tried to project calm and act like I knew what I was doing.

"We now have a change of plans for this evening's service," I announced. Before they could all start asking each other what was going on, I continued on, "due to unfortunate circumstances that have arisen, making it impossible for us to use the Bima tonight, We need to leave the Sanctuary. Please make your way to the Chapel instead and bring your programs and prayer books with you."

I knew I would be bombarded with some questions concerning what these "unfortunate circumstances" were, but I was hoping I could put off answering them until the police arrived. I wasn't sure they would be too happy with me announcing what we'd found. Or rather, what I thought we had found. I was pretty sure that man was dead, and it had probably been murder. None of us had felt for a pulse because we were all afraid to touch him. I also thought I knew who it was, but since we hadn't seen his face clearly, I certainly didn't want to set off any rumors on the off chance I was wrong.

I grabbed my own things, including the candy, and headed over to the Chapel with everyone else.

Chapter 4
Pivoting

When I got to the chapel, I saw all the kids huddled together in one corner. Some were shaking, others looked like they were on the verge of throwing up, and a few were joking around as if nothing unusual had just occurred. The adults were all whispering to each other, and my paranoia spiked a bit when I realized a number of board members and important donors had come to the service and seemed to be huddled together too. Were they going to blame me for this? Or use it as an excuse not to renew my contract? I had to concentrate on my breathing to stay as calm as I could.

My elderly but spritely friend, Dani Chaco, caught my eye and gave me a discrete smile. She wasn't Rachel, but it was nice to have her here. Maybe it was due to her training as a social worker, that Dani was so good at being a steadying presence and a voice of sanity and clear-sightedness when navigating synagogue politics. Plus, I knew she'd give me a chance to process the events of this evening during our next walk'n'talk in a couple of days. We didn't have any particular schedule we followed, but a couple of times a month Dani and I would take long walks, usually on one of the area's many nature trails, and we would process synagogue and world events as we walked.

Dani had to have been in her late seventies or early eighties, but you would never know it to look at her. She was one of the most active people I knew, taking advantage of all of the bike paths and walking trails around the area to exercise her body, and attending all sorts of adult education classes to keep her mind sharp. She probably had better stamina than I did, and I was a good few decades younger. Yet, she also seemed to somehow emit kindly old auntie-type vibes.

Despite our difference in ages, I enjoyed our walks together and I really appreciated her unwavering support. I was glad that she was a regular both at services and at my adult education programs, but also she had let me know in no uncertain terms she supported me. It meant no matter what happened next, there was at least one person here who was in my corner. Well, two, but Mina was at the door waiting for the police. (I didn't count Rachel because she's a few hours away, but I knew I could call her anytime and I'd feel like we were sitting next to each other wrapped in blankets on the couch with a plate of fresh chocolate chip cookies between us.)

It must have taken even longer than I thought to get everyone settled in the chapel. It seemed almost as soon as everyone was seated and the whispering had died down, Mina walked into the room followed closely by two policemen. They looked so much alike I wondered if they were brothers or cousins. Perhaps they were but that wasn't important at all. What mattered was they were here to help.

Everyone froze as the police entered. Then the clamor started up. "What's going on?" "Why are the police here?" "Does this have something to do with why you rushed us out of the sanctuary?"

Glancing at the police for permission, I once again tried to create some order out of the chaos. Fortunately, most of the people in the room had grown up with the traditional call for silence used in camps, youth groups, and religious school classrooms. All I had to do was say "sheket bevakasha" (which means quiet, please) for them to respond with a hearty "hey" and silence.

"Thank you," I began. "The police are here because the children and I discovered something unsettling on the Bima. They haven't had a chance to go over to the sanctuary yet and assess the situation for themselves, so I'm going to go out on a limb and guess that no one can answer all of your questions yet. We will, however, be able to tell you something about what you can expect to happen now." I glanced over at the policemen and one of them stood up to speak.

"Thank you all for being so cooperative. My name is Detective Tara, and I've been called in to figure out what is happening here. We'll be able to tell you more once we've had a chance to look for ourselves, but for now, we'd really appreciate it if you could all stay here until we have a chance to talk with each of you to figure out what happened."

Hannah tentatively raised her hand and asked, "what about our class service and dinner? Are we going to have to reschedule that for another time?"

Detective Tara waited a moment before answering. "What does your class service entail? Will you have to leave this room?"

"No," the class chorused. "We can do it here. Like we practiced the other day," said a few of the kids. Sam nodded in agreement and his face shifted to an anxious expression rather than full-blown panic.

"In that case, I think going ahead with the service is a fine idea," said Detective Tara. "I would need you to stay here until I can come back and talk with each of you individually anyway, and this sounds like a good use of your time while we" he gestured to the other policeman, "and our team do our jobs."

I thanked the detective and turned to the students. "You've all worked so hard," I said, "and I know waiting around can be hard. Having this opportunity to take in the peace of Shabbat in the midst of this chaos and anxiety is the best medicine this rabbi can imagine right now."

Mina gestured to the police officers they should follow her, and I got the kids situated in front so they could each be seen as they led the prayers (and other pieces) they had practiced. Voices were definitely shaky at first, but, as I had suspected, the further we got into the service, the steadier they all looked and sounded... even Sam.

The adults, too, seemed less anxious as the service progressed. I saw smiles and heard a few giggles as the members of the class explained how the Psalms with which we open the Shabbat service are a lot like Now'n'Laters because we are supposed to use these prayers to think about the week we are leaving behind and focus on just being present in the now. Doing that, they said, also helps make the later a bit sweeter because we start it more peacefully.

"That is a clever way to look at these prayers," Dani couldn't help interjecting. The faces of the students responsible for that one beamed.

As the service continued, another student explained the prayer "L'cha Dodi" in which we welcome the mystical Shabbat bride reminded them of Sunkist fruit gels. They shared they came up with this connection because those are the candies we throw at a bride and groom to wish them a sweet life together. That got a chuckle from a few of the adults in the room, who I suspected were remembering their own experience of having these candies flying at them from all directions.

Other students stood up and explained; in order to represent the love discussed in the "V'ahavta" prayer, they had chosen Hershey's kisses, and for the flexibility we have to add our own thoughts and prayers to God during the Amidah they discussed the combination of flexibility and structure in prayer.

I could see the family members, Dani, and the handful of other congregants were impressed by the students' creativity and clear understanding of what they were doing and saying. A few of the board members had a generally genial expression so no one could ever really know what they were thinking or feeling. But I didn't let that inscrutable expression throw me off my stride.

I was proud of what a good job all the students had done with leading the prayers and sharing these thoughts and observations in a way that showed they understood the essence of these prayers we say each week. I was happy to have the class break into the candy and distribute it among everyone there. As an added bonus, the tension in the room had diminished significantly.

While we were busy praying and listening to Kitah Kochavim, the police were busy over in the Sanctuary. None of us even realized the two officers who had responded first had been joined by a whole host of other people. Based on my vast knowledge drawn from TV dramas and novels, I presumed these other people were the crime scene techs. As it turned out, it didn't take the original two police officers long to determine the person on the Bima was, in fact, not just dead, but murdered. I had suspected as much based on the way the body was lying down and the pool of blood, but I really appreciated the police didn't interrupt the service to share any of this while they conducted their initial examination.

Mina had let all these police personnel in through a door far enough away from the Chapel that it didn't disturb our service at all. She later told me she sat in the back of the Sanctuary and watched them scurry around in a purposeful manner. They used tweezers to put things into little baggies that they sealed into a black case with a built-in lock. One person walked all around the body, the whole Bima, and even parts of the Sanctuary taking lots of pictures. She also thought some of the others put on funny-looking glasses. I figured they must have been using the glasses to see things like infrared or ultraviolet or whatever.

By what felt like divine intervention, the crime scene techs and coroner's people finished up their work in the Sanctuary at almost the exact same time we finished our service in the Chapel. I noticed Mina come in and quietly stand at the back of the room flanked by the same two officers who had been there when we started. After the usual weekly announcements, praise of the students, and thanks to everyone for being there, I added a special thank you to the police for both their prompt response and for letting us conduct our service without interruption. Heads turned so everyone could see for themselves that the detectives had returned to the room. Detective Tara made eye contact with me. His direct gaze unnerved me slightly. Then I realized he was trying to get my attention to signal he and his partner wanted to address the group.

"Hi! In case you forgot, my name is Detective Tara," he began, "and I am grateful you all did such a marvelous job staying here and letting us do our work in the other room. I know you are anxious to know what our examination of your Sanctuary revealed, and you probably are wondering what will happen next. There's not a lot I can tell you at this point, but I can confirm there was a dead body on the Bima." He turned to me and in a loud whisper said, "that is the correct term, right." I smiled and nodded so he continued, "as of now, we are treating this as a murder investigation, so I will need you all to stay here a bit longer until I, or one of my officers, has a chance to speak with you individually."

"Murder!" everyone flinched and was started exclaiming and speaking over each other mumbling as to who it could be.

"Do we have to stay in this room? Or can we go eat? I'm hungry!" grumbled Ethan.

Ethan's comment was followed by a chorus of, "I'm hungry, too" that was overpowered by another voice.

"I don't want to stay in a building with a dead body! I'm a cohen," declared Abner Kleinman, Ethan's father. "A cohen isn't supposed to go near a dead body! This is a violation of my rights!" his voice rose in volume with each word and so did his body.

"Please calm down, sir," said Detective Tara in a smooth, commanding tone. "The deceased is no longer in the building. He is on his way to the morgue. As far as I know, no one's rights have been violated except for those of the dead man."

As Abner visibly calmed and returned to his seat, a voice called out, "so, who died?"

Suddenly, you could have heard a pin drop as everyone turned to stare at Detective Tara.

"The deceased was identified by Mina as Leonard Steinberg. We will, of course, need to verify that identification so we can notify his next of kin and proceed with our investigation."

I could hear the kids whispering to each other, "who's Leonard Steinberg? There are no Steinbergs in our class..." a voice piped in cutting him off "Dummy, he's the synagogue president..."

Before the clamor of questions and reactions could resume in force, Detective Tara said in a voice that did not require a microphone to be heard at the back of any room, "It's my understanding you all had planned to share dinner together here in the Social Hall. We need you all to stay so we can talk to each of you, but I don't see any reason to keep you from your dinner."

"Even if you hadn't originally planned on staying," I added, "we have plenty of food for everyone." That's when I realized I didn't see the new person amidst the congregants. I frowned slightly, but didn't say anything. I'd tell Detective Tara, but I wouldn't dwell on it. I needed to stay focused and help move everyone along to the Social Hall.

"Before you all go enjoy your dinner, I want to let you know the rabbi is letting us use her office for our conversations, so when it's your turn to talk with us, that's where you'll come."

"You're not going to talk to my kid unless I'm there!" roared Sam's father with a lot more vehemence than warranted.

"Thank you for bringing that up," said Detective Tara. "Obviously, what these kids have to say will be very important to our investigation, but we have no intention of violating any of their rights.

Just like those of you who are adults in this room, these teens have the right to remain silent and not answer any questions.

They also have the right to an attorney, just like you do. However, there is no legal requirement for us to include parents in our questioning of these young people, and we will respect their decisions regarding who they wish to have in the room while they are talking with us."

There was a loud snort, but no further push-back from Sam's dad or anyone else. I tried to take mental notes of how smoothly the detective had been able to diffuse Sam's father and be able to sidestep a possible contentious confrontation. I wanted to be able to do that just as effortlessly as Detective Tara.

"Thank you all for your cooperation," he said as he stepped aside for me to announce what everyone was to do next.

"Let's all head down to the social hall so we can do kiddush (the prayer over the wine), make motzi (the blessing over bread), and enjoy the lovely meal prepared for us by the caterers. This certainly has been a memorable class service, and these kids have worked really hard. They have shown courage, fortitude, and a love of sweets." I was glad that bit got a few chuckles.

"If it's OK with you, Detective Tara, I would like to suggest speaking with the students first so they will have at least some possibility of relaxing a bit tonight."

"That sounds like a fine idea to me," agreed the detective.

"Sam, would it make you feel better to be the first to talk with the police?" I asked, figuring given his temperament, he was the one most likely to get overly anxious while waiting his turn.

"I'd rather go second, if that's OK,"

Emma raised her hand. "Can I go first? I don't think I can eat just yet. It was all just too horrible!"

It was hard to tell whether her words were a sincere expression of her emotions or whether they were what she thought she ought to be saying in this situation. Either way, no one objected or insisted on being first.

"Of course," said Detective Tara. "Do you want anyone to come with you?"

"I think I'll be OK by myself. But could my mom sit outside the office in case I need her?

"That sounds like a wonderful idea."

Chapter 5
Emma

Despite her insistence on being the first to talk to the police, Emma really didn't have very much of any substance to say in aid of the investigation. As anyone who knows her could have predicted, most of what she told Detective Tara was repeated variants of how awful it was to see and be so close to a dead body. She had no idea who Leonard was and was unclear on why a synagogue even had a president.

The only substantial piece of the puzzle Emma shared with Detective Tara when asked if she knew of anything unusual that happened prior to the class service.

"You mean like the big fight we heard last week?" she asked wide-eyed with an innocence that wreaked of insincerity.

"There was a big fight last week?" asked Detective Tara. "What can you tell me about it?"

"It was during our class. It was really loud. We couldn't hear any words or anything, but we heard lots of banging and loud noises, like shouting. I had to go home with Sherry Kahn instead of with my usual carpool."

"Who is Sherry Kahn? And what happened to your usual ride?"

"Sherry Kahn is our neighbor. My mom said Sherry is a board member. She's here a lot for meetings and services and stuff like that."

"Is she here tonight?"

"Yeah. She was sitting next to my parents."

"And last week she gave you a ride home after your class, but she's not usually the one who drives you. Did I get that right?" asked Detective Tara.

"Right. I usually go home with Hannah and Ethan because we all live near each other. But last week, after all of the shouting, a few of the parents came rushing through the door to our class, grabbing their kids and taking them even though class wasn't over yet. They all seemed super upset."

"Was there something special about these particular parents? Were they already in the building?"

"Well, Rabbi Whyte said they were all board members. The other upset adults, too. But why would anyone on the synagogue board be so angry anyways?" asked Emma. "I thought all they did was ask for money. That's why they call my family so much."

"I think they do a bit more than just ask your parents for money. But I'm glad you told me about how angry they were and that they had a big fight. That's really important information."

Emma's chest puffed up with pride as she flounced out of the room.

Chapter 6
Sam's Story

Sam opted to have his parents in the room with him when it was his turn to talk to police. Although he managed to sound somewhat confident while leading the service with his classmates, being forced to talk to police had his knees and tongue forgetting how to function properly. I was a little surprised Sam wanted both his parents with him, given his fear of his dad's temper. But, it wasn't my call, so I shrugged it off.

When Sam and his parents went to talk with Detective Tara, it made me think about conversations I had in the past few weeks with Avital, Dave, Mina, and Leonard. There were definitely some strong feelings among these folks, including animosity (or even hate). I hoped Sam and his parents were sharing their view of recent events so Detective Tara could get a sense of the bigger picture and not just leap to conclusions.

I hope they shared with Detective Tara the way I had needed to address Sam's panic over the thought of the class service. Originally, I was a little worried about what they were going to say.

Sam's dad, Dave Rosenberg, had some really strong ideas about what kids should be learning in Religious School, and even how the learning should take place. He was of the old school, desks in rows and endless drills and recitation of prayers. He believed in tests and the importance of decorum. Needless-to-say, he was not open to hearing about the latest research and best practices in education.

I believed Jewish education should be both meaningful and fun. It should ignite a spark to want to learn and do more. To Dave, I knew, my classes looked chaotic and undisciplined. But I thought my methods were effective at reaching my goals and I was not about to revert to Dave's old-fashioned ideas about school.

Having worked with Sam before, I knew he was anxious about getting up in front of everyone and leading prayers. That's why my heart had been bursting with smiles to see how engaged he had been in class once we began preparing for the service. It's true he didn't leave with a huge smile wrapped in adrenaline and excited looking forward to the class service. But it looked like he might be starting to actually build some type of personal connection with the prayers. His face had returned to a normal color rather than a sickly green. In my mind, that counted as a big win.

I recalled how I had picked up the phone and as I dialed, I said my own prayer that Sam's dad would not quash those feelings out of the poor boy by insisting on more focus on rote repetition.

I let out a breath I hadn't realized I was holding when it was Avital, Sam's mother, who picked up the phone. After we exchanged pleasantries, she got to the point.

"When I asked Sam how Hebrew School was yesterday, and what he'd done, he said 'nothing.' I know that's a typical pre-teen type of answer, but..." she trailed off.

"Are you're worried about Sam?"

"Well, I thought I remembered something about a class service coming up, so I asked him about it. He told me it was canceled, but I think he was lying." She let out a small sigh. "He tried to say it wasn't really mandatory so he won't have to go. I didn't want to push him too hard because he seemed upset, but.... Well, I thought I should check with you. If you hadn't called me, I would have called you later today."

"I'm really glad we managed to connect. Yes, Sam's class does have a class service coming up, and I expect everyone to be there unless they are actually sick," I responded with a light chuckle that seemed fake even to me. I went on to tell her the date and time of the service, but I could tell there was still something else on her mind.

"Oh thank you," Avital uttered the words nervously. "Now I have it on my calendar, and I just have to figure out how to deal with the fact Sam lied. Normally, he's such a good, sweet boy. It's not like him to lie...." she sounded completely flustered.

"Do you have any idea why Sam was lying to you?" I asked gently.

"Well.... I think he's nervous but, I don't know what he's nervous about. My husband will make him practice the prayers, so he should be fine."

I didn't think Sam's father pushing him would help the situation. In fact, I was fairly certain it would make things worse for

Sam. I tried to be careful with my response. "Sometimes, it's not about the prayers.. Does Sam have stage fright in other situations?"

"I don't know," she practically wailed.

That seemed a rather extreme reaction. Maybe her husband was making things more stressful already. I took a few minutes to calm her down, reassuring her lots of kids are nervous before leading services. I also made sure to mention some local resources that can help kids with anxiety, in case there was something bigger behind Sam's attempts to avoid participating in the class service. Sam's mother calmed down but still seemed at a loss as to how to work with Sam on this issue. She begged me to "talk to him and fix this" during his Bar Mitzvah lesson that afternoon. God help me, but I agreed. I really did want to help Sam.

Typically, people think of two main things when it comes to a Bar, Bat, or B' Mitzvah (the name is different for boys, girls, and non-binary thirteen–year-olds, but the ceremonial aspects are generally the same). There's the "religious" piece, where the child leads some of the prayers, reads from the Torah scroll, and gives a short speech. Then there is some type of party to celebrate this milestone has been reached and the child is now a full-fledged member of the Jewish community. I work with each of the kids to help them learn their individual Torah readings, since we read a different one each week. In addition to practicing the prayers and learning to chant the Torah reading, I talk with them about the meaning of the day and of the piece of Torah they are learning.

That day, as relieved as I was to have talked to Avital, I decided that rather than wait for Sam's dad's take on all this, I should try to get ahead of whatever was going on. So, I bit the bullet and dialed Dave's cell phone number. A male voice picked up. "Hello? Who is this?"

"Dave, it's Rabbi Shachar Whyte."

"Rabbi?!? What's wrong? Don't tell me! Sam made a mess of his last lesson."

"No, not at all, Dave," I tried to project calming thoughts through the phone line. "I'm sure Avital has already filled you in on our conversation earlier and I just..."

"AVITAL!!!"

Not at all sure I hadn't lost my hearing, I spoke up again, since it seemed I had inadvertently stuck my foot in my mouth.

"AVITAL!!!"

This one was followed by a much softer female voice "What's wrong, Dave?"

"WHY IS THE RABBI CALLING ME?!?!?"

"Mr. Rosenberg. Dave. You're right I am calling about Sam."

"Tell me what my kid did. I'll take care of it. Kid won't know what hit him."

"Please, no hitting," I felt the panic and the fear creep into my voice slightly. "I just wanted to clear a few things up with you."

He huffed. "Fine. I'm listening."

"First of all, I want to let you know Sam did a really good job in class yesterday, but I am a bit worried about him."

"I knew it! The kid's an idiot!"

"Not at all, Dave. Sam is quite bright, and very sensitive."

"Now you're calling my boy a sissy?!?! How dare you! When I tell everyone…"

"No, Mr. Rosenberg, that's not what I'm saying at all," feeling like I was vacillating between cowering under his verbal assault, trying to use my tone of voice to put out a fire, and giving a stern rebuke to a child who was refusing to listen. "This morning, when I spoke to Avital, it was in regard to Kitah Kochavim's upcoming class service. I wanted to make sure you were aware Sam is doing well and will do even better with your support than with any negative incentive."

"Are you trying to tell me how to parent my kid? You are out of line!" his voice grew into a growly roar.

"Not at all, Dave," I said, trying to remain calm and open to learning about his point of view. "I would never tell you how to parent your child. I'm just letting you know my observations so we can work together to help Sam succeed."

"OK." Dave's voice immediately lost the loud, threatening aspect it had taken on just moments before.

If Sam's family had shared those conversations with Detective Tara, it probably wouldn't impede the investigation. It was the conversation that came next that seemed more ominous in retrospect.

I told Dave I hadn't talked with Avital about my understanding that Leonard had made some threats about Sam not being allowed to celebrate his Bar Mitzvah. I wasn't sure if there were any words in Dave's growl that tested the lower range of my hearing or not. So, I gently forged ahead. "I will get this straightened out. Sam will celebrate his Bar Mitzvah just like the rest of his classmates."

I recalled that had elicited a *'hrmph'*. Fine. Maybe you can knock some sense into that thick skull of Leonard's. I don't like him messing with my boy." Dave growled.

Remembering that last remark now, in light of finding Leonard's dead body, what had seemed like Dave just blowing off steam at the time, now sounded much more threatening. I cringed inwardly. I was going to have to share this with Detective Tara, wasn't I? This was going to be awful! It was just hitting me. It was highly likely the murderer was a member of the congregation, possibly even someone with whom I'd had a lot of contact. Before I let my mind start wandering down that black rabbit hole, I refocused my thoughts on Sam.

Then, I suddenly remembered a conversation I'd had with Mina a few weeks ago. It was the morning after Kitah Kochavim and I heard the big fight. I came in to work to find Mina was already at her desk. As usual, I stopped to chat for a few minutes before going to my own office. She asked how the previous night's class with Kitah Kochavim had gone, and I started rambling on about what a good class it had been and how animated they had been when they left. She was making all the appropriate encouraging sounds, but I knew she wasn't actually listening to a word I was saying.

Then, I noticed the expression on her face and felt my shoulders tense. There was something about her expression that put me on my guard and I immediately wondered whether she had already heard complaints from a parent or whether some other problem had come up with the date or the food for the dinner after the service. I realized I was being paranoid. It had been a good class. The kids seemed to have fun, and I thought they were making good personal connections when they were thinking creatively about the prayers.

"I'm sure it was," Mina said, trying to reassure me, but her manner just increased how nervous I was.

"Mina, you're killing me here," I said. "What's wrong? I don't think you were just being polite, or expected me to say what I did. So, what have you heard?"

As the one who answered the phones and sat by the door, Mina knew a lot more about the internal politics and interpersonal issues in this synagogue community than anyone else. I was glad we were friendly and could share workplace woes with each other.

"What's wrong?" I asked.

She leaned toward me and her colorful feather earrings practically brushed my cheek as she quietly admitted "Everyone is yelling at me to *'take care of it'* and I don't know what I'm supposed to do!"

"What are you talking about? I'm confused. Back up and start again, please."

Now, I hoped she was sharing these same thoughts with Detective Tara because they took on a more sinister tone in light of Leonard's death. She told me she had heard at the last board meeting Leonard made some comment about how we shouldn't be letting kids even schedule a Bar or Bat Mitzvah if they haven't learned how to read Hebrew properly yet. And someone else had chimed in insisting all outstanding dues be paid as well.

Mina was upset because Leonard had called her and told her she had to tell Sam's family they aren't allowed to have his Bar Mitzvah. She had told Leonard that was not her job, but in light of finding his corpse, it made me realize there were a lot of people who thought Dave (and maybe Avital) had a strong motive to kill Leonard.

I hadn't realized until that moment how much of my time lately had been focused on trying to help Sam in one way or another.

But it was easy to take the burden off of Mina. I told her, "That was definitely the right thing to do. It is not your responsibility to get involved in this. It's also not the president's decision who gets to have a Bar Mitzvah here, especially without talking to any of the clergy! Did Lilith also try to get you involved in this mess?"

"Not yet, but I wouldn't be surprised to hear from her, too."

The case against Dave seemed even stronger when I remembered Mina had told me "Then, the phone rang and it was Sam's dad! He was hopping mad, too! He screamed at me for a good 5-10 minutes then slammed the phone in my ear without me having said anything."

I told her I was so sorry she had to deal with this! Sam's dad is scary when he yells, but I keep telling myself deep down he's really just a teddy bear. I've never seen any evidence of him hurting Sam or his wife. Or maybe he's like Jekyll and Hyde and knows how to not leave visible bruises. I haven't quite figured it out and I've known him for years now.

I had thought the rest of our conversation that morning was much calmer.

In retrospect, I realized Mina also had had issues with Leonard.

"Thanks. Just being able to tell you about it has brought my heart rate back down to normal," Mina sighed.

"Not sure I did anything, but I'm glad you're feeling better and more centered now. What a day! Want a piece of chocolate?" Mina gratefully accepted.

"Anything else I should know?" I asked Mina while dreading the news there was some other major catastrophe for me to handle.

"Bulletin deadline is tomorrow. I have your flyer for youth programs but still need an article from you." Mina smiled.

"I promise to get it to you before I leave today." I sighed.

Then she told me she and Leonard had often struggled over the bulletin. He was always on her to get the bulletin out on time, but he was also always late to submit his letter and to give his approval on the final draft. And Mina had heard rumors that Leonard had started telling the board she couldn't handle the job.

I sympathized. I didn't really know what else to say. Now I was worried.The fact I was had my own troubles with the president of the board and Mina was well aware of them would point to me as a strong suspect. Both Mina and I had talked about our fears of losing our jobs at least three times a week for the past few weeks.

I remember I grabbed my mail and headed to my office to take a few calming breaths. By the time I met with Sam that evening for his Bar Mitzvah lesson, I had pushed all thoughts of my own insecurities and worries off to the side and was able to focus on the adolescent in front of me.

"Sam, did you know your mom and I talked with each other today?"

"No. Why? I've been practicing, I swear."

"I'm glad to hear that, and I sincerely hope it's true. I know I've already told you this, but it's the practice you do in between our sessions that will really help it all stick in your brain. But the call wasn't about whether you've been practicing or not."

I could feel Sam's unease fill the momentary silence.

"Why did you tell your mom the class service had been canceled? You know that's not true." It took some gentle coaxing, but

Sam quietly admitted his fears and I reminded him practice builds confidence.

After my pep talk, Sam reluctantly agreed to do a little chanting for me. Once he got into the swing of it, his shoulders came down from next to his ears. I may even have caught the beginnings of a grin when I commented on how much progress he had made on one of the prayers.

Thankfully, even though she arrived early, Sam's mom knew how to stand quietly in a place where Sam wouldn't notice. I was sure if he realized he had an audience, even the slight relaxation I'd seen would vanish and he would start stumbling over words. While Sam was packing up his papers, I stepped out into the hallway to greet Avital and ask how she was doing.

"I'm fine, Rabbi, thank you," she automatically replied. "No, that's a lie. I'm worried about Sam," she whispered.

"Are you worried about something in particular?" I ushered her slightly further from the doorway toward my office to make it harder for Sam to overhear.

"I still don't know what to do about Sam's lying," she whispered to me. "It's just not like Sam to lie to me," she wrung her hands. "He's a good boy, really, he is."

"I know. Sam is a great kid."

"I'm afraid Dave's going to be upset. He already thinks Sam is lazy and stupid, and that's why his Hebrew isn't better."

"I can assure both you and Dave, Avital, Sam is working really hard. Hebrew and prayers come harder to some kids than others, and Sam knows a lot more than either you or Dave realize."

"Really?"

"Really. I have a feeling you may have heard some of that just now."

"I swear I didn't mean to eavesdrop or anything. But I was just so worried…"

"It's OK. I won't tell Sam you had any doubts about him or his progress."

"Then why did he lie to me about the class service?" Avital wailed in frustration, confusion, and exhaustion.

"As I said before," I whispered calmly, "Sam is really making great progress. He knows a lot more than he lets most people see, but I think that's because his anxiety takes over when he knows there are other people listening to him or looking at him."

She must have felt slightly guilty for listening to our lesson and not recognizing how bad her son's anxiety had become. Holding back the water I saw glistening at the corner of her eyes, Avital hastened to assure me she wasn't trying to imply in any way she thought I wasn't doing my job. And she'd say as much to Dave, too.

Until she said that, the thought hadn't even crossed my mind. Plenty of parents arrive early to pick up their kids or sit nearby in the building while their kids have lessons. And I could understand why Sam's mom felt the need to eavesdrop. But now that Avital had planted the thought in my head there might be some people who felt I wasn't doing a good job, or there was some reason they didn't trust me, it was hard to rein in the swirling doubts and worries.

Thankfully, Avital's next words helped bring me back to the present and soothed my zooming thoughts for a bit. "I think you're doing the best you can with Sam. After all, I know how difficult working with him can be! So I really do appreciate what you are doing. I just keep hearing such different stories and assessments of Sam from everyone."

I murmured something indistinct to let her know I was listening and sympathized with her.

"Thank you!" said Avital, letting out a sigh.

***

Indulging in comfort foods full of carbs and sugars while watching my current favorite TV show helped me to unwind from the day. *'There's nothing like a good murder mystery,'* I thought to myself as I licked the last drops of ice cream off the spoon. In hindsight, I can say real-life murder is not fun and entertaining like the TV shows I watched.

I really hoped the Rosenbergs were being honest with Detective Tara about what happened at that crazy contentious board meeting and the fact Leonard had kept threatening not to let Sam have his Bar Mitzvah.

Chapter 7
Boiling Over

Ethan and his mom, Elaine, met with Detective Tara together. While I had half expected a facade of bravado from Ethan, it was clear this whole situation unnerved him more than he was willing to admit to his classmates. It was interesting his father, Abner, didn't join them and instead opted to speak with the police on his own. It made me wonder whether he had something he was trying to hide from his wife and son. In fact, when I thought about it, I was pretty sure I recalled hearing him raising his voice at that particularly contentious board meeting. Maybe it was a good thing he wasn't sitting in on Ethan's conversation with the detectives.

Thinking about Ethan's parents and that board I recalled a conversation Mina and I had the morning after the meeting.

"I really don't know why this is so controversial!" I vented to Mina. "Everyone knows it's freezing in winter and kids are sitting in classrooms wearing their winter coats and mittens. If the inspector comes and sees we have electric heaters in the preschool rooms, we could lose our license."

Timid in the face of my vehemence, Mina said, "I think everyone wants to fix the temperature in the building, but no one can agree on which company or system to use, A few board members keep telling me I need to call this place or that and see if they'll lower the price. That's not part of my job. And I don't report to those board members. But, if I don't do it, they'll just keep calling and getting on my case."

"You have a point, but I thought one of the board members works at a company that does this stuff."

"Not a board member, I don't think. But I think you might be right there is a congregant in this field..." mused Mina. As if she were in a cartoon, I could almost see the lightbulb go on above her head. "Isn't this what Elaine Kleinman's company does?" She tapped a few keys on the computer before confirming, "Yup. Here it is. Elaine's Electric and Heat. They sell boilers and electric heating units. The company was started by Elaine's father, because he always intended for her to take over after him," she paused, "but, he's got to be in his 80s and he is clearly still the one in charge."

In light of Leonard's death, I now wondered if it was possible Leonard was angry that Elaine wouldn't just have her company donate what we need. If so, it would be a reasonable assumption he had directed his anger and frustration toward Abner that evening since Elaine isn't a board member and wasn't at the meeting. That could have been what Abner was so upset about and why he wanted to speak with the detectives alone.

I remembered the adage that money is one of the main motives for murder. I wondered how Elaine felt about this whole question of the synagogue's boiler. Was she angry at being passed over? Or at having been bullied by Leonard to give SBM a better deal? But, for all I knew, it was possible she wasn't mad at all and she didn't want to mix her work life with her synagogue life.

Chapter 8
Time to Go Home

I didn't know how the interviews had gone for everyone, but based on the conversations I overheard as I walked around the Social Hall greeting people, praising the students for a job well done, and making small talk with everyone who had come that evening, it sounded like the police had asked all of us pretty much the same questions. They had taken down everyone's names, addresses, phone numbers, and anything else they might need to get in touch and follow up with anyone later. It also sounded like everyone had been asked to account for when they arrived at the synagogue and what they had been doing for an hour or two before services. The police wanted to know everyone's relationship to Leonard, and if they knew of anyone who might have hated Leonard enough to kill him, but it seemed like tonight's conversations had been more about constructing a timeline of everyone's movements rather than about motive.

By the time dessert had been set out, the students had all gathered around one table. I noticed, as I had expected, they each had plates filled with brownies, cookies, lemon bars, and some even had a little bit of fruit. What was unusual was the amount of food sitting uneaten on those plates and the fact they weren't shouting over each other. They had their heads huddled as close together over the table as they could, so I was fairly certain they were comparing notes about their conversations with the police.

I sat down as quietly and as unobtrusively as I could to try to hear what they were saying. I got as far as figuring out some of them told the police about the fighting we had heard on the night of the board meeting, and others hadn't. A few students were really worried that talking or not talking about that night could get them into a lot of trouble. They all had worried looks on their faces, but the conversation came to an abrupt halt when one of the girls spotted me and gave me the stink eye.

I forced a smile and a half wave. "I didn't mean to intrude," I said. "I just came over to check how you are all doing, and you seemed to be in the middle of a very intense conversation."

The looks they gave each other told me I was right, but they did not want to talk to any grownups about it.

"I'm going to leave you to chat and enjoy those delicious-looking desserts," I assured them. "But I want you all to know you don't have to wait until class to reach out to me. You can phone me or email me."

They nodded, and I left them, my mind already racing with thoughts of what to do with them in class to help them deal with having been the ones to discover the murder. I had enough faith in myself to know I would figure something out. Whether the parents, police, Lilith, and the remaining members of the board would agree with what I was planning remained to be seen. I knew my priority was doing what I could to take care of these students. Like most, if not all, of my colleagues, I had gone through crisis and trauma training. We all knew they could befall our communities at any time. Even with security on our doors, we were all too aware of the reality of shootings, bomb threats, and graffiti experienced at synagogues around the world. We were trained on how to react to these types of threats. But no one had ever covered what to do if you find a dead body on the Bima at a service that kids are scheduled to lead.

Chapter 9
Lilith and the Antisemite

I know the police were trying to speak with all of the others in attendance that Friday night before talking with me, so I tried to be as patient as I could be. Everyone else had already finished dessert and I had just put the last dish away. The building was starting to empty as those who had already given their statements were allowed to leave. Meanwhile, I looked around for a book to read as I settled into one of the chairs in the chapel. I had a feeling I would be waiting a long time since it was Lilith who was giving her statement right now. She was no doubt repeating herself and doing her best to get them to reveal more than she did.

In fact, if I had to guess, I would say Lilith was trying to focus Detective Tara's attention on the antisemitic call that had come through the other day to draw attention away from the members of the synagogue. Even though I had been the one to talk to the guy, not her, I'm sure she would tell the story as if she were the only one privy to the facts.

Thinking back to the day that disturbing call came in, I recalled I had barely hung up the phone when I noticed the light for the second line was flashing. Within seconds of me replacing the receiver on the cradle, Mina buzzed to tell me there was another call on the line for me. Her voice made it sound as if she was pale and shaken.

"What's wrong?" I asked her. "You sound like you've seen another bat," I said in an attempt at levity. Last month, Mina had been looking for a file in the synagogue's attic and had been scared by a bat that flew right past her face. She had run back down to her office, shut the doors, and frantically told me to do the same. After consultation with four different board members, Mina was told to call the exterminator and have them take care of what was being referred to as "the bat problem." And apparently it wasn't just one, the exterminator found a few bats to remove. I'm glad I never saw any of them.

"No, no worries, not another bat. But this might be even worse."

What could be worse? Did we have a rat problem too? This was an old building, so it could be any number of things causing Mina to panic like this. She wasn't exactly known for being calm under pressure.

"While you were on the phone, the other line rang," she began.

"OK," I said, drawing the syllables out in puzzlement. "I see there is still someone on that line, either waiting for you to help them with something or hoping you'll transfer them over to me. That's not so strange or upsetting, but it does mean we don't really have time to chat right now."

"It was what the guy said I'm worried about. You'll hear when you talk to him yourself. I don't know who he is, but he was saying all sorts of terrible things about the Jews, threatening violence against us, and demanding to talk to you."

"OK, transfer the call to me. After I've talked with him, I'll come over to your desk and let you know what I think."

"OK," came the reluctant reply.

A heartbeat later I found myself saying into the mouthpiece of the phone, "Shalom. Synagogue B'Kol Makom. Rabbi Whyte speaking. How may I help you?"

"I don't want your help!"

"Then, may I ask why you're calling?"

"I thought it was only fair to give you one chance," replied the menacing voice.

"Chance? To do what?"

"Leave and stop spreading your filthy lies and propaganda."

"I'm sorry, but I don't know what lies and propaganda you're talking about, sir."

"Don't try to get cute with me! I saw that Israeli flag on your building. Ha! Yeah, that's right, I know where your building is," I could hear the sneer even through the phone. I wasn't sure how to respond. Usually I was glad to know people could find us, but right at that moment, I wasn't so sure.

"And I know you and that old guy you call a president are the worst of the lot. Taking everyone's money so you can buy yourself fancy new clothes and cars."

OK. Clearly the caller was referring to Leonard Steinberg, and not to the president of the United States. Though, to be fair, they were both old white guys. I tried to keep my voice calm and steady, like I'd been taught to do when faced with an angry congregant or a potentially threatening situation.

"Sir, I think you may have been misinformed. I don't have fancy new clothes or an expensive car. The only money the synagogue collects from members and outside donations is used to cover basic operating expenses and to allow us to help others. Furthermore, ideas about Jews and money are harmful stereotypes that have been used to spread fear and hatred. We don't go around just taking people's money. Like anyone else, we get paid for doing our jobs." I was a little surprised he hadn't interrupted me yet.

"Even if I believed you, Rabbi, which I don't, I still know you and that other guy are brainwashing kids so they become Zionist monsters killing innocent Palestinian kids."

If I wasn't before, I was now officially in over my head here. It was clear that logic would not get through to this guy. "It sounds like you and I see the world very differently, sir. I'd be happy to meet with you to help correct some of the misconceptions you seem to have picked up about Jews. If you give me your email address, I'd even be happy to send you some links you might find informative."

"You think I'm stupid?!?! I'm not gonna give you my email address so you can try some of your hoodoo on me!"

"No, of course not," I tried to sound as soothing and non-threatening as I could.

"I know where you are. You and that old guy what's-his-name. You can bet I'll come find you and teach you a lesson soon."

With that, there was a sharp click, and he was gone. I sat with the receiver in my hand, staring at it in shock. When my lungs forced me to gasp, I realized I must have been holding my breath. My brief paralysis lifted and I put down the phone. I stared into space vacantly for a minute or two before remembering Mina was waiting to hear from me. My legs shook as I made my way to Mina's desk, trying to figure out what I was going to tell her.

As I feared, she began to panic. "I know you say he didn't say anything about me, but I sit closest to the door. What if he really does come and starts shooting or plants a bomb?"

I gulped. Clearly Mina needed me to at least seem calm, collected, and in control here, even though my insides were shaking like Jello. "OK. Remember what we were taught in that training on threats? I'm going to need you to call the police and the chair of the security committee to let them know.

"Right. Call the police and the security committee. I can do that."

Even though I knew before talking to Mina, I would have to personally be the one to tell Leonard about the antisemitic caller, especially with the threats that clearly seemed to be referring to him, I couldn't hide my slight grimace at the thought. As I recalled that conversation, I wondered whether it was possible the caller had gotten into the building and carried out his threats. Maybe the detectives would be able to trace that call and hopefully they would agree with the way we handled the situation.

"We probably should check to make sure all of the doors are actually closed and locked. We do have a couple that stick sometimes," I reminded Mina.

She agreed and went off to make her calls and check the doors. It looked like she felt better now that I had reminded her of specific tasks that needed to be done in a situation like this. I wish I could say the same about myself. We'd had a good relationship with the local police for years, and I was sure they'd send someone over to check the building. Hopefully there would be more frequent police drive-bys for the next few days. I wasn't quite sure what the security committee would do, but I left that up to them to figure out.

I remembered taking some deep breaths and steeling myself to call Leonard that day. (I hoped I didn't need to share that information with the police now that he was dead.) I hadn't finished entering Leonard's number when the phone rang. Since I knew Mina was going around checking doors, I answered it. I should have known better and continued dialing Leonard's number.

If I hadn't picked up the phone, I would have had to listen to a ridiculously long voice mail message and then I would still have to suffer through the same conversation. So, maybe I saved myself a tiny bit of agitation by picking up the phone right away.

"Oh, hello! I'm surprised to hear you answering the phone. Is Mina not in today?" a familiar voice asked.

"She's here, just away from her desk at the moment," I responded.

"I thought maybe she had gone home already," Lilith Polshani said. Lilith was a board member with whom I spoke at least three times a week. Often more. She oversaw the education committee and seemed to be involved in almost everything else, too.

Frequently, she knew about things before I did, which was a bit of a sore spot for me. She was on at least 5 different committees I knew of, and who knows how many others she was either involved with herself or was informed about by other people. She managed to often position herself as the kind, welcoming face and voice of Synagogue B'Kol Makom, even though she didn't have any official standing to do so. But everyone let her do so because she always seemed so kind and caring when you first met her.

In fact, when I first arrived here, she had a huge fruit basket delivered to me. And she always got me brownies, which are my favorite, when she went to the bakery. Unfortunately, she is long winded. Rather than a 20 second email requesting a call back, she'll leave messages that take over two minutes to listen to in their entirety. If someone else could convey a message in a 5 sentence email, Lilith's would be at least 5 paragraphs long. Any phone call with Lilith that lasted less than 45 minutes was a small miracle.

I realized Lilith was waiting for me to say something and I picked up the thread of the conversation again. "Why would Mina go home so early? She's very dedicated to her job, and I've always found her to be reliable."

Lilith interrupted, "Of course she is. She usually picks the phone up promptly. When you answered the phone instead of her, I got worried that someone in her family was sick or she had a doctor's appointment she forgot to tell me about in advance. I was worried that this morning's events had upset her so much she had gone home to recover. She must have been really rattled by that phone call. Do you know anything more about who made it? Or where it came from? I wanted to make sure you are both safe and to find out if the police think it was a credible threat or not. But Mina hasn't left?"

Comments like this are why I now assumed Lillith was telling the detectives all about this phone call even though she hadn't been directly involved.

How could Lilith know about the threatening antisemitic call so fast? I had only just hung up a few minutes before, and I wasn't even sure if Mina had called the police or security committee yet. I know I hadn't even had a chance to finish dialing Leonard's number. Somehow, Lilith seemed to have inside knowledge about just about everything that happened at the synagogue. I wondered if she was a spy or had hidden cameras or bugs all over the building. Or, crazy as it seemed to even think it, could she have somehow been behind the call? She did seem to have a way of getting other people to talk, while revealing very little about herself or things she knew. I shook my head. *"Ridiculous,"* I told myself. I was fairly certain there were no secret nanny-cams around the building. What would be the point of spying on our humble little synagogue anyway? And why would anyone orchestrate an antisemitic attack against their own synagogue?"

I must have paused slightly too long, because Lilith started pelting me with more questions about what actions had already been taken. When I was finally able to get a word in edgewise, I gently said, "wow, news sure does travel fast. Mina just left my office to go check all of our doors. I don't know if she's had time to make any of those calls or not, but there definitely hasn't been enough time for the police to do any sort of in-depth investigation."

"Of course. That does make sense. I'm glad to hear Mina is checking all of the doors. Do you think the preschoolers who are in the building are safe? Maybe we should evacuate them to the church or have their parents come pick them up now."

"I think either of those scenarios would make the parents panic more. We have safe shelters and evacuation plans that are already approved, and unless the police say otherwise, I think it's better for the kids to have as normal a day as possible."

"Right. We definitely do not want the parents to panic. Would you like me to send an email to the parents to let them know what is happening? Or maybe a letter can go home in each child's backpack today. I would be happy to write it for you. I know you must be busy."

"Thank you for the offer, but I think it's too premature to decide on next steps."

"Synagogues all over the country have been getting threatening calls, but the calls haven't actually been followed by any physical threats. We can't let ourselves be vulnerable just because we are not in a major metropolitan area...."

She went on in this vein for a while, coming up with theoretical worst-case scenarios and questions of how I planned to keep the kids safe. Thank goodness this was not a day when Religious School met, or we'd be going in circles about whether we needed to cancel classes or not.

Thirty minutes after the phone had rung, I finally managed to extricate myself from the conversation. A record! I wondered if Lilith would also tell the police about the disagreements she and Leonard seemed to be having lately or if she would spend her time trying to point fingers elsewhere.

Chapter 10
My Turn Begins

Once Detective Tara had spoken with everyone else in attendance, it was my turn. As if talking to the police about a body found on the Bima wasn't uncomfortable enough, it felt especially odd to walk into my office and find someone else in my chair, forcing me into one of the visitor seats. Fortunately, before things could get too awkward, Detective Tara began by thanking me profusely for the use of my office. Then made an offer I never would have expected.

"Would this conversation be easier and more comfortable for you if we switch seats?" he asked.

I stared at him for a brief moment. "No, it's OK. I'll be OK in this chair," I said. "It's a little weird, but then again, so is pretty much everything about this evening."

"To tell the truth, I have been pretty impressed with how you've handled yourself and how calm you have seemed this whole time," Detective Tara said.

"I have not been nearly as calm on the inside. As a rabbi and an educator, I've had to deal with a number of highly emotionally charged situations, and I know how much my own reactions can potentially trigger others. So, I've had some practice projecting a calm I don't really feel, Detective."

I couldn't read Detective Tara's face to see how he was taking my response. Did he appreciate my openness and honesty? Or did he think I was using some type of excuse to hide guilt? I really hoped he believed me. I wasn't sure I could handle an attack on my ethics and values system that being a suspect would entail. Instead, he jumped right in with his questions. "Right now, I need you to help me get a sense of the sequence in which things are typically done on Fridays. Why don't you start by filling me in on your day, Rabbi Whyte," he said in a friendly, yet business-like, tone of voice.

"Sure," I agreed. "It was really like any other Friday up until, well, you know. Or at least, like any other week when one of the Religious School classes is helping to lead services," I continued to fill Detective Tara in on my morning, which had included replying to emails, making sure the program pamphlet was ready for services that evening, and checking to see if we had everything we needed for Religious School on Sunday morning. Even though I didn't need to prepare a sermon for Friday night, I still had to write one for Saturday morning. Now, however, that seemed like a wasted hour and a half because I was pretty sure I would need to address the discovery of the body on the Bima.

Detective Tara made a sympathetic noise. "I don't know how you do that,"

"Do what?" I asked.

"Write two whole speeches every week then stand up and deliver them to a whole congregation. I'm much better with one-on-one conversations."

"It's part of what I was trained to do," I shrugged. "And it's gotten easier the longer I've been doing this."

"And after you wrote your sermon, what did you do next?" he prodded, moving my narrative along.

I told him Mina had made copies of the "program" that let everyone know who would be leading which prayers and included some of the extra readings, songs, and explanations the kids had written up. I also checked in with the caterer to see how the dinner preparation was coming along and was on the phone for a while.

I continued, reiterating how after being on the phone for so long, I felt like I needed to get up and move for a bit. I figured that was the perfect time to put the programs in the Sanctuary and check everything was all set for the service.

"So you were in the Sanctuary this afternoon?" Detective Tara asked, leaning slightly forward in his chair.

"Yes, of course," I replied. "How else would I know if we were ready or not?" It took a minute for my brain to catch up with my mouth. "Oh!" I gasped, having just realized the importance of what he was asking. "Actually," I added, "I should probably tell you that I even went up on the Bima to put some of the programs there for the students to have access to."

"When you checked the Bima then, did you notice anything out of place?" he interrupted.

"No, it all looked normal. No shoes or legs poking out or dead body, if that's what you mean," I answered.

He cracked a wry grin, acknowledging my attempt at levity. "Fair point. I hoped that was the case. But I'm trying to get both a sense of the setting and the timeline. The coroner will help narrow down time of death, but it's nice to establish a timeline of people's movements as well."

That made sense. I had already figured out the murder had to have taken place between when I set up for the service and the service itself.

"What is normally on the Bima on Friday afternoons before services?" asked Detective Tara.

I was certainly in my element here! The idea of teaching this man who seemed to vacillate between terrifyingly authoritative and as cuddly as a teddy bear was something I would love to do! Not only was I happy to list the items normally found on the Bima, I offered to make a sketch or show Detective Tara around. I was even willing to give him a crash course introduction to Judaism. The longer we talked, the more relaxed I became and my excitement over the possibility of a reason to spend more time with this intriguing man even overshadowed the nerves and forebodings of evil brought on by Leonard's murder. Detective Tara flashed me a kind smile and I sensed there might be some interest there, but then he said that for now, all he needed was a quick run-down of what items should have been at the scene to determine if anything had been either added or taken away.

Explaining what items were on the Bima before I left the building for a couple of hours was fairly straightforward. "The ark was closed and locked, and there were cups and grape juice for the end of the service. There was also a pair of candlesticks, which were off to the side because we weren't going to light them with kids on the Bima. I worried too much about the disasters that could ensue from that combination. There was a neat stack of papers Mina had printed out with the weekly announcements, a list of people for whom we were saying a prayer for healing, and a list of those who had passed away at this time in previous years."

"Thank you," he commented. "And did you notice if any of those items you just mentioned had been moved between when you put out the pamphlets and when the body was found?"

I shook my head and shrugged my shoulders regretfully.

"That's OK. If anything comes back to you later, please let me know. I'm sure you had many things on your mind in that moment."

"Yes. It still all feels completely surreal. Plus I'm used to seeing the same things on the Bima each week, and even though they tend to be in roughly the same places each week, they do get moved around."

It was when Detective Tara asked, "Can you walk me through what happened when you found the body?" that I found my answers becoming slightly flustered. I was able to relate the overall sequence quite easily, but remembering what each student said and my impressions of each of their expressions was much harder. Detective Tara calmly and gently prompted me as I tried to untangle what felt like a very chaotic moment.

"Other than the shoes and legs, did you notice anything unusual either in the room or in how anyone was behaving?"

"No, nothing. Other than the kids being frozen like they had seen Medusa. The lack of their usual exuberance was eerie."

"You lifted up the corner of the cloth to get a peek at the rest of the body, correct?"

"I did. I know you aren't supposed to touch anything at a crime scene, but I wanted to know if the person was hurt and whether we could do anything to help. But, he was completely still, and I was pretty sure I could see both blood and brains." I shuddered at the memory.

"I'm sorry you had to see that," said Detective Tara in a very kind voice that made me want to hug him and be held in return. I was working hard to put a quick stop to that daydream when he asked, "did you recognize the victim?"

"No, I didn't. I couldn't really see his face and I didn't touch him or try to turn him over or anything." I gave an involuntary little shiver.

"But would I be right to presume now that he's been identified as Leonard Steinberg, you know who that is?"

"Of course," I replied, "he was the President of the synagogue."

The detective nodded, making a mental note of some sort. I was grateful he didn't jump right into asking about my relationship with Leonard, though I knew I wouldn't be able to avoid that forever. Unfortunately, my reprieve didn't last more than a few minutes. First, Detective Tara asked a few questions about whether I knew of anyone who might want to kill Leonard.

This was a tricky question for me to navigate because I didn't want to point fingers or speak ill of anyone, especially not congregants who actually held the future of my employment in their hands. At the same time, I wanted to do everything I could to aid the police in their investigation. A murderer had to be brought to justice, and people needed to feel the synagogue was safe. As somewhat of a compromise or balance between these differing priorities, I set out to explain Leonard's often abrasive personality and an overview of the connections and interactions with everyone who had been at the service to the best of my ability. I tried to keep my tone neutral, relating facts and trying to steer clear of anything resembling judgment or inference. It was harder than I thought it would be, especially once it came time for me to talk about my latest interactions with Leonard. I tried to steady my nerves with some four square breathing, because I knew once the police learned about my recent interactions with Leonard, there was a good chance I'd suddenly be a lot higher on the suspect list.

Chapter 11-
My Last Interactions with Leonard

I explained to Detective Tara that I felt like I had been on the phone a lot recently, between the antisemitic caller and then Lilith. Before continuing, I checked to see that Detective Tara knew what I was talking about with these references.

"Yes, Lilith filled us in on this antisemitic phone call you received." In a neutral voice he added, "for someone who was not on the call itself, she seemed to know an awful lot about it."

I sighed. "I don't know where she gets all of her information, but she did ask me and Mina for whatever details we could provide. I completely understand if you need me to go over it again with you after I finish answering your question about Leonard."

He nodded and gestured for me to continue, so I resumed my story. I told Detective Tara I had barely hung up the phone after that antisemitic call and the post-call conversation with Lillith, taken a calming breath, and steeled myself to once again dial Leonard's number when the synagogue president himself strode in and took a seat.

Detective Tara tried to hide his surprise as I described this unexpected visit. Leonard Steinberg had tried very hard to project an air of wealth and authority. He always wore a pressed suit and shoes polished to such an extent they reflected his white and gray neatly trimmed hair. When he entered a space, the air in the room seemed to have condensed into something heavier and more dignified, as if just by his very presence he assumed control of the room and everything in it.

I told the detective that before I could invite him to sit or tell him about the antisemitic call, Lenord had strode over and sat down in one of my "visitor chairs in a clear demonstration of entitlement mixed with subtle bullying, at the same time saying, *'There's a problem'*.

I knew that was never an auspicious start to a conversation. Now, with Leonard dead, it felt even more ominous as I told Detective Tara about what had happened.

I tried not to show Leonard how flustered I was, and wondered whether we'd had a meeting scheduled that I had forgotten. Or whether, like Lilith, he had already heard about the antisemitic threats and wanted to work out a plan with me?

I told Detective Tara how I had responded by saying "yes, antisemitic threats are always a problem. But, we have policies and procedures on how to handle them. It's a problem for which we are prepared, and I was actually in the middle of calling you to fill you in on the incident..."

Leonard had not followed my lead. He had waved my words away as if I was speaking nonsense, telling me he wasn't talking about the call I had gotten. He wasn't, as he had put it, "worried about some antisemitic crackpot."

I had still thought Leonard ought to know about the specific threats made against him. Not that he was about to let me get a word in edgewise.

"Your contract is up for renewal this year," he had stated. Before I could say anything, he had continued. "You know we like you and your family. But this isn't about liking you. No, this is about measurable outcomes. You haven't grown the size of the school and

I've been told the kids haven't learned all of the prayers. I don't think you have the votes you'll need for a new contract. Let me know if you decide to resign."

Having dropped that bombshell, he left my office as abruptly as he had entered. I hadn't even managed to tell him that the antisemitic caller had specifically mentioned Leonard in his threats.

"You must have been pretty angry with Leonard for doing that to you," mused Detective Tara.

"Not exactly angry," I replied. "It's more that I was flabbergasted. Or stunned. I knew there were tensions seething beneath the surface of interactions among the synagogue leadership which had already resulted in a certain amount of upheaval. But, I had, perhaps naively, thought myself immune to the political machinations going on behind the scenes". I explained that sure there were things I was trying to improve, but I could not single-handedly reverse the multiple nation-wide trends that had to be dealt with. A lot of my friends and colleagues had also been complaining about low enrollments, a lack of willingness to practice at home which led to poorer mastery of prayers and other material, and the increased difficulty finding qualified teachers or, truthfully, any teachers at all who could commit to the weird hours our classes met, among other things.

I explained this all to my education committee and the synagogue board. So I was confused by what Leonard had meant when he said he didn't think I had the votes. Were they going to fire me because I didn't have the magic solution to reverse nation-wide trends? My brow wrinkled even in the retelling, I wondered how they could vote on my contract without having done any type of full performance review in years. At least I had a few solid allies, like Dani Chaco, that would tell me the truth about what was going on behind my back.

I was sure whatever she had said while being questioned was quite carefully worded. I told Detective Tara Dani had been putting a bit of a bug in my ear insinuating Lilith didn't quite have my back the way I thought she did. But there was also the possibility, I shared, that she did have my back and that was part of what she and Leonard had been fighting about.

I told Detective Tara I knew I needed to get back to work and finally face my emails, but it was really hard to concentrate after the president's drop in. I thought if I arranged a "walk'n'talk" with Dani, I could settle down enough to get back to some of the other work still waiting for my attention. But I was still too on edge to focus on conquering the tasks on my to-do list. So for an immediate boost, I came up with a flimsy excuse to go visit the students in the preschool. I should probably let the teachers know about the antisemitic caller, who for some reason I was rapidly starting to think of as "Jim Bob." Plus, the children's enthusiasm and antics would be sure to cheer me up and chase away the thoughts still circling like a windstorm in my brain.

Detective Tara smiled and shared that he also found children's laughter and antics a good antidote to feeling blue, tired, or overwhelmed. Enjoying a small spark of warmth at sharing this love of children with Detective Tara, I resumed the recitation of my latest dealings with Leonard. I shared that it wasn't until the following day that I was finally able to tell Leonard about the threat against him. Even though Leonard never hesitated to ambush me in my office, as I dialed the phone, it occurred to me this was my first time actually calling him.

I remembered the feeling I had after exchanging polite yet wary greetings with Leonard, I had held my breath and jumped right in, as if this conversation was a pool of cold water I was being compelled to enter.

I filled Detective Tara in on the details of that conversation. I shared I had thanked Leonard for taking the time to talk with me since he had left before I had the chance to talk to him about the antisemitic call in any detail. Leonard had sounded gruff, terse, impatient, and bored on the other end of the line. He was quite clear to me that Lilith had already told him about the call, and Mina already talked to the security committees, so, I wasn't wasting my time repeating what others had already told him.

I honestly told Leonard I was very glad Lilith and Mina were able to fill him in on both the phone call itself and on what we are doing to be extra vigilant right now. But I told Leonard they don't know everything. I was the one who actually talked to this man. He grudgingly told me he was listening and I told him that in addition to the general antisemitic threats, the caller had also mentioned him as a particular target.

Leonard didn't take that news very well. He insisted he didn't know any violent antisemites. He accused me of being mistaken and of overreacting, telling me the caller was probably just trying to scare me. Then Leonard had told me I was making a big fuss over a trifle instead of doing the things I was hired to do. Even though I was fuming inside and felt like a volcano about to erupt, I remained calm and rational as I told Leonard the antisemitic caller sounded pretty serious, and did specifically not just talk about the president of the synagogue but he also gave enough descriptive details that it was very clear he was talking about Leonard.

Having imparted the information about the antisemite, I forged ahead and told Leonard we also needed to talk about Sam Rosenberg's Bar Mitzvah. Leonard sounded gruff and blustery when he asked what there even was to talk about. Leonard had been quite forceful in sharing his belief that the kid's not ready. He doesn't know his prayers and his parents are behind on dues and fees.

I don't know if Leonard really heard what I told him next, or if it mattered now in light of his death. I had told him Sam was actually progressing quite well and had learned a lot during our individual sessions. Then, I admitted to Detective Tara, I had gathered up my courage to rebuke Leonard. I tried to soften it somewhat by telling Leonard I knew how much he did for this community. Then I firmly told him it wasn't his job to make a decision like this about who can have a Bar Mitzvah. It's mine.

That's when Leonard argued that it was his responsibility to keep SBM solvent, when a family is behind on dues, they don't get the same use of our building and staff. I agreed that he and the rest of the board were tasked with overseeing the financials. Then I sternly stated that didn't give him, or any of the board members, the right to prevent someone from celebrating a lifecycle event.

I exhaled. It felt tense even in the retelling. I'm not certain, but I thought it looked like Detective Tara was fighting an urge to clap for me.

Chapter 12
Walk 'n' Talk

I didn't think telling Detective Tara about my walk with Dani after these nerve-rattling interactions was relevant to the case, so I didn't mention it. But, for the sake of completeness, I'll share it with you now.

I was really glad Dani had stopped by the synagogue for our planned walk'n'talk. My thoughts were such a tangled mess ever since dealing with the antisemitic caller and Leonard's bomb drop the previous day, that it was hard to focus on all of the other things going on. Fortunately, the weather that day was perfect fall weather for a small town in upstate New York. The sun was enhancing all of the color on the trees and they looked as if they could be posing for a portrait. The temperature was perfect for wearing just a light cardigan that would be discarded after just a few minutes of walking. And there was a scent in the air unique to autumn. I took a few deep breaths while I watched Dani park and get out of her car.

"I'm so glad this worked out!" I told her. "I needed to get out of my office and spend some time outside today."

"I thought you might need it. It sounds like you've had a lot to deal with lately."

"What have you heard?"

"I saw Mina at the sports shop. She was getting some fishing gear and some extra feather lures to make those earrings of hers. Anyway, I was there because I think it might be time for me to get a new helmet."

I didn't really want to engage in polite conversation about Dani's shopping trip. Fortunately, an inquisitive "and?" was all it took to shift the conversation. I don't think Dani really wanted to talk about shopping either.

"She told me about that awful call you had!"

"I take it Mina gave you more details than what was shared with the board, because you should have also gotten the message that was sent to board members."

"I did, but I was concerned about you both. Mina wouldn't say much. You know she's professional and doesn't go spreading gossip.

But her description did sound more scary than the message shared with the board. How are you holding up?"

"It's been a rough few days."

"I'm sure. And it's not just the threat, is it? What else is going on?"

I sighed and told Dani about my recent conversations with Leonard and that I was also sorting things out for a family.

"That sounds like a lot," she commented.

"It is," I sighed again. "But I know I can help the family." In retrospect, confiding that my bigger concern was figuring out how to deal with Leonard might not have been the best idea. But how was I supposed to know he would soon be found dead on the Bima?

By the time I had finished telling her about Leonard's surprise visit and the very real threat that I would be out of a job in a couple of months, we had reached a small bridge overlooking a stream. We paused to stare down at the water swirling past rocks and tall grasses. "No ducks," I commented. "Maybe they've already migrated for the winter. It was cold a few days ago..."

I know you've been really worried about this contract renewal," Dani remarked.

"I don't even know if Leonard was just sharing his own thoughts and opinions or if a lot of people feel the same way... And it's not like Leonard has ever been very chatty..."

"I agree Leonard has always seemed brusque and hard to read... But you should know you have your supporters too."

"I think Lilith has my back. We've spent a lot of time working together." That elicited a barely concealed grimace from Dani. "I know you disagree. You don't think I have Lilith's full support. Since you're on the board, are there any insights you can share with me about what's going on?"

"I wish I could. I'm not surprised to hear there are people who would rather bring in someone new, but I also know I'm not the only one who supports you and has your back. I'm not sure who stands where, though. I tried to talk Leonard out of doing anything about your contract without first doing some sort of survey or evaluation. Unfortunately, Leonard has never listened to anything I've had to say. Especially when it comes to anything important or the running of SBM."

I let out a very deep sigh. I hoped Dani would have some insider knowledge to share but that clearly wasn't the case. I would just have to muddle through the best I could. Our talk turned to other topics as we headed back to the synagogue. As we reached the front door, I thanked Dani for listening, closed my eyes to take in one more deep breath, and turned to face the rest of the day.

Chapter 13
The Big Fight

While I didn't tell Detective Tara about that walk with Dani, I did make sure to get his approval regarding the message that I sent to the congregation to inform everyone of Leonard's death.

I don't write (or send emails) on Shabbat, but I knew as soon as Shabbat was over, I would need to send a message to the entire congregation. I'm sure the news had already spread like wildfire through the congregation. So, the wording of the official message I was about to write would be crucial. It could influence the fate of my contract, could uncover schisms in the congregation, and could impact the police investigation.

Leonard had not been an easy person to get along with, as plenty of people can attest to, but I knew my message still had to be filled with the usual platitudes about how he'd be missed. I had talked to the police before they left on Friday night, and I was given the green light to share the news of Leonard's passing and also the fact that this was a murder. They just strongly cautioned me against revealing any details the police might want to use to help them catch the killer, such as where the body was found, anything about a possible murder weapon, or any speculations I might have about what had happened. Since Leonard's body wouldn't be released to his family until after the autopsy, there were no details about a funeral to be shared yet, but I was given permission to hold a memorial service whenever the family wished to do so.

After wracking my brains about what to say as the sky grew darker and darker on Saturday, I finally figured out what to write shortly after three stars had appeared in the sky and Shabbat was officially over. I could feel my body tense as if bracing for impact when I hit send on the following:

Subject: Tragic Loss on Friday Night

Dear Members of the Congregation,
It is with profound sadness and heavy heart that I come to you today to share the devastating news of

the passing of our board president, Leonard Steinberg. Leonard was found murdered in the synagogue on Friday evening, and we are grateful for the rapid response and aid of the police. Our entire community is in shock and mourning over this loss, and I know you will all do your utmost to assist the police and one another as we navigate this challenging time.

Leonard was an esteemed member of our congregation and a dedicated servant of our community, and his absence will be deeply felt. Details regarding his funeral and information about shiva will be sent as soon as they are available. In the meantime, please keep Leonard, his family, friends, and our community in your thoughts and prayers.

Resources on how to talk to children about scary and tragic events like this are available on the synagogue's website, as are some sources adults may find helpful.

If you or anyone you know needs support or assistance during this time, please do not hesitate to reach out to me. I am here for you, and we will support each other through this shocking tragedy.

With deepest sympathy and heartfelt condolences...

I signed it and hit "send." I hoped getting out that message would allow me to release the breath I'd been holding. I did let out one fairly large exhale, but my shoulders didn't have any time to loosen up before I realized I still had to deal with Religious School in the morning.

I always hated coming up with appropriate programming after crises in the community when I knew families would be on wildly different pages about what they were willing to have shared with their kids. I had tried talking to the parents about how impossible it is to keep our kids in any sort of insulated bubble. One way or another, kids will, unfortunately, hear about synagogue shootings, antisemitic attacks, violence in Israel, and any number of other terrors, injustices, and other difficulties in the world. So, while I would reserve the bulk of the processing time for the students who had been there on Friday, and other individuals who needed what little guidance I was able to provide, I would not ignore the elephant wearing a kippah who would be joining us in the morning.

Fortunately, there were no plans for any of the students or teachers to go into the Sanctuary for any reason, and the police were doing some extra drives by the building to see everything was safe and secure. Mina had recruited a couple of synagogue members she trusted to help monitor the doors with her. I figured it would be quite easy to reassure the parents their children would be safe and would not inadvertently see something horrific at the crime scene.

That Sunday morning after Leonard's body was found on the Bima, Detective Misha Tara called to ask me about the big fight some of the kids had talked about when they were giving him their statements Friday night. I gave him more of an explanation than he was probably looking for, but he didn't interrupt or complain.

I began my account from when I was setting up the chapel for Kitah Kochavim. For class, I had put all of the chairs into rows instead of a circle. On the walls of the hallway that led away from the chapel past some offices, I had hung up a bunch of posters. This was usually a pretty observant group of kids, so I had turned out the lights in the hallway until I was ready to reveal the posters and the activity that accompanied them.

Once all of the kids were there and had a few minutes to chat with one another, comparing notes about teachers etc. and projects they were working on, I rolled over the white board, still covered in the prior week's lists, and began the class with a discussion of the Shabbat service they were going to be leading.

Detective Tara didn't interrupt to ask how Friday night's service was different than what the class prepared.

I gently reminded the students they were going to be expected to incorporate their innovative ideas from the prior week with some of the pieces that were "fixed."

I could see that despite the work we had done together over the course of the last week, Sam once again looked like he was turning a bit green. I knew from prior years some of the kids in this class, including Sam, were not particularly confident to get up in front of friends, parents, and general congregants to speak let alone lead parts of the service. I realized before I continued with the lesson planned, I needed to take a few moments to assuage some of their fears.

I tried to reassure them, and to ignore the groans when I said we were going to practice now. "I know some of you are worried about the class service," I began, and repeated what I had told Sam during his lesson, "but in all of my years of doing this, I can confidently say no one has ever died on the Bima in the middle of their class service either here or at any of the other congregations where my friends work."

"Not yet," I heard Sam mumble. "Doesn't mean it won't happen this time."

I realized Sam was convinced he was going to die up there right in front of everyone. Either God would strike him down for not knowing what he was doing and for making fun of this whole prayer thing, or he would die of embarrassment because he had absolutely no clue how to say the words or what tune to sing.

It wasn't true of course. I knew (or at least thought I did) Sam wouldn't die or be struck down. I also knew Sam and anyone else who was anxious would only feel worse if I didn't quickly move the class into the evening's activity. A huge groan went up when I passed out the siddurim (prayer books), though the class did perk up when I told them it wasn't going to be a regular practice, but a bit of an experiment. I told them they had to pay attention to what they were thinking and feeling while we practiced. They looked a bit skeptical, but opened up the prayer books anyway. Everyone started perking up more when we started to add in some of the tunes, thoughts about candy, and other interpretations they had worked up the previous week.

Part way through I stopped them and told them to follow me. I could hear their whispers of curiosity as I brought them into the large Sanctuary and up onto the Bima. They looked at one another a bit askance when I told them to pick up with their practice from where we had left off in the Chapel.

Usually, we pray in one place. We don't pick up and move to a different room in the middle of a service. I could tell from the puzzled glances they gave each other I had gotten their attention. But, before Ethan Kleinman, the class's biggest troublemaker and one most likely to derail class, could say anything, Hannah Berman stepped up to the microphone and began singing. From there, the rest of the practice went smoothly.

After we practiced the last prayer of the service, Emma Silverman raised her hand and asked in her typical whine why we had just done that. By "that" I knew she was referring to switching rooms, but Hannah leapt to my defense quite confidently before I could explain. "We're supposed to learn something from it, of course."

"Duh. But what was that supposed to teach us? Why did we do it?" Emma said to Hannah with condescension dripping from her lips.

I wanted to let the suspense build for just a tiny bit longer as I made Emma actually clarify what she wanted to know. But, I knew I better step in before they all began arguing. Still, instead of giving Emma a direct answer, I handed each student a pack of post it notes and a pen. Seeing Hannah's hand shoot up, I hurried to explain their task was to explore the way the setting can impact how close we feel to God. I watched as understanding lit up their eyes while I gave the rest of the directions for the activity.

They would have time to walk up and down the hall where I had put the posters and react to the pictures they saw there. They should think about whether it looked like a good place to pray and whether they had ever felt God or spiritual in a place like the one pictured. They should record their thoughts on a sticky note and stick them onto the wall next to or around the picture. I was really curious to see what they would have to say! I had included pictures of forests, bodies of water, classrooms, small chapels, big sanctuaries, a zoom screen, living rooms, and more.

We headed to the hallway. Students chatted and began to spread out among the pictures, we heard loud noises coming from above us. It sounded like a mixture of banging and shouting. It was so unexpected all the chatter stopped immediately.

My students gave each other nervous looks, and both Sam and Emma looked like they were scoping out places to hide. Ethan, of course, was assessing what items around us might make good weapons. Isaac Weiss maintained his posture of cool nonchalance. Before everything could dissolve into chaos, I rushed to calm them down and keep them focused on the task, if possible.

The noises sounded louder, angrier and my main concern was ensuring the students of Kitah Kochavim were safe and calm in these unusual circumstances.

"It's OK," I told them. "The synagogue board is having a meeting in the room above us. I'm sure the noise we heard is just coming from their meeting."

"Sounds like they're having a fight," said Sam with a slight tremor in his voice.

"Nah," replied Ethan, regaining his cool. "I recognize that voice. That's my dad. He just gets loud and sometimes when he's all worked up about something, his face gets red like in the cartoons."

"Does smoke come out of his ears?" asked Isaac with a teasing grin.

"No, stupid. He's a real person, not an actual cartoon character. Duh!"

"Why would anyone on the board be so angry anyways?" asked Emma. "I thought all they did was ask for money. That's why they call my family so much. Because helping others is our responsibility since we have so much when others have so little."

I considered explaining more things the board was responsible for, but then we heard what sounded like furniture being tossed about and the words "over my dead body!" then a slamming door. Everyone froze in shock then started talking all at once.

Despite the initial set-up having gone so well, I knew there was no way I would get the kids to refocus on the discussion and activity I had planned. Who could think about how different places influence how we feel when we are praying with so many scary noises coming from the room above, where the board was meeting.

I was in the middle of a vain attempt to get the kids to return to the chapel when a couple of board members stormed the room, each grabbing a kid and propelling them out the door. Everyone else just stood there in shocked silence for a brief moment before all of the kids started talking at once.

"Who was that who grabbed Emma?" asked Hannah with concern. "That wasn't her mother! I know her mother!"

"Should we call the police?" asked Ethan. "Was that a kidnapping? Did someone kidnap Emma?"

"Why would someone kidnap Emma? It's not like they could get a big ransom for her or anything" said Ethan.

"You asking to be kidnapped?" asked Isaac in a lazy drawl.

"Of course not, you idiot!"

"She was not kidnapped," I finally managed to say. "Sherry Kahn gave her a ride home as they live on the same block."

Ethan and Hannah's "Oh." was somewhat subdued.

Then Ethan forged ahead. "So Emma wasn't kidnapped. Fine. But did you see the way Sam's mom just grabbed his arm and yanked him out of here?"

"I've never seen Sam's mom drag anyone anywhere," said Isaac. "She's more likely to stand there wringing a tissue in her hands and loudly sighing and making comments about how we really ought to go." Heads nodded in agreement.

"Plus, she's never left me behind before and I thought Sam's mom was supposed to drive me home today!" continued Isaac. I reassured him I would make sure he had a ride to get home safely.

"My dad, on the other hand..." said Ethan as his dad clomped into the room with a scowl on his face as he motioned to Ethan that it was time to go. We had lost half the class by this point, but the kids still had a lot of questions. As did I.

"Why were they so angry?" piped up a timid voice.

"Will they be OK?" asked Hannah.

"Who? The kids or the grownups?" wondered Isaac.

"What happened up there?" asked a voice made small with fear.

"I thought grownups knew how to calm down! They're always telling us to breathe when we get mad!" huffed Hannah.

Since I didn't have any answers for them, I softly began to hum a melody I knew would be familiar to the kids. I had to prompt them a little and invite them to sing with me, but they did so readily enough, even if it was quietly and a bit of reluctantly. Once all of the conversation had stopped, I was able to get them to sit down. I'd love to say we were able to spend our last few minutes of class having a deep, profound conversation. But all I could do was reduce the panic level before the rest of the parents arrived to pick up their children. And, as I thought she might, Hannah's mother graciously agreed to drive Isaac home, even though it was a little bit out of her way.

After I finished telling all this to Detective Tara, he nodded slightly, which I took as a sign that this lined up with the other accounts people had given him.

I then told him how it was with a big sigh of relief that I began to clean up all of the posters, sticky notes, pens, prayer books, and other paraphernalia that had been used that day. I could not wait to get home, put on fuzzy slippers, and curl up on the couch. But, when I heard voices coming from a room down the hall, I knew my fuzzy slippers and couch would have to wait. I was too wound up to even consider passing up the opportunity to gain some insight into what was going on here.

I convinced myself I wasn't exactly eavesdropping. They were in a public spot, and their voices carried without me doing anything more than slowing the pace at which I was doing what I normally did to close up the building after class.

Detective Tara fought a smile while gesturing for me to continue sharing what I had overheard.

I did my best to fully repeat the conversation I'd heard word for word, and it only felt slightly odd to be recreating the words of a dead man so I continued repeating the recent past events for Detective Tara.

"How do you think that meeting went?" said a voice dripping honey that barely concealed the bitter undertones.

"Things got way out of hand, but I can take care of it," replied a gruff voice.

Clearly the board meeting was a disaster. I couldn't believe the shouting and chaos. I'd heard animosity and voices raised in passion before but this was next level!

"Out of hand is one way of putting it," came the voice I had identified as belonging to Lilith. "I would love to hear your insight into what happened and what exactly you plan to do about it now. What happened tonight was unacceptable. If it's too overwhelming for you, maybe we need to call an emergency vote to add a co-president!"

"I don't need a co-president!" came the strident voice belonging to Leonard. "I told you I can take care of it and I will!"

"Yes, but how? You have so many things to deal with right now. Sam's Bar Mitzvah, Rabbi Whyte, the boiler... Let me take something off of your plate. I'd be happy to help speak to Sam's family for you," she said in that saccharine-sweet way of hers. "I was already going to be talking to Avital this week..."

Having been the recipient of similar offers of "help" myself, I knew her offer of help was both simultaneously genuine and a cover for some sort of hidden agenda. I wasn't sure what that hidden agenda might be. Was she on Leonard's side, trying to prevent Sam from celebrating his Bar Mitzvah? Or was she planning to make herself out to be the helpful friend and advocate with Leonard being the evil villain.

"I can do it!" Leonard's voice was even louder and more strident than before.

"Of course you can. I'm just offering to help make things easier for you." Someone with less experience talking to Lilith might mistake this for a genuine offer of help, but I sensed some unknown ulterior motive behind her words.

She continued, like water gradually wearing a hole in a rock, "Before I talk to Avital, let me make sure I understand correctly where things stand with Sam's Bar Mitzvah. You want to forbid him from having his Bar Mitzvah here both because you don't think he's capable of leading parts of the service and doing his Torah reading, and also because his family is behind on their financial obligations to the congregation.

"That's right," Leonard had admitted grudgingly and I could already predict how this would go, so I moved slightly farther away, to clean up that area.

Then I heard Leonard shout "We don't want the kid to embarrass us! That's on Rabbi Whyte, not the Rosenbergs!"

I inched closer to hear Lilith's reply. "You are right. We don't want to highlight the way in which our Religious School has begun failing under the direction of the rabbi," said Lilith in a voice that dripped syrup. "I know you remember we used to have 4 times as many students when our children attended classes here. And all of the kids could read and recite prayers fluently by the time they reached Bar or Bat Mitzvah age."

I wish I had been more shocked to hear Lilith throw me under the bus so blatantly like that. But I knew I couldn't dwell on that now if I wanted to hear the rest of this conversation. So, I did my best to shove it to the back of my mind to haunt me when I tried to go to sleep later.

"Right. Religious School enrollment is definitely down from 5 years ago. I thought the rabbi was going to bring in all of those unaffiliated Jews and staff the school with highly experienced teachers," Leonard said with a mixture of disdain, disappointment, and something else in his voice. "She isn't living up to our expectations. Now her salary is having a negative impact on the budget."

"So, why didn't you call for a vote regarding the rabbi's contract? I thought you were going to do that tonight,." Lilith probed.

Wow. I had thought Lilith wanted me to stay. She always said things to imply she was super supportive of me and the things I was doing here. It was always Leonard who gave the negative, disappointed, unwelcome vibes. I needed to reassess what I thought I knew about the power dynamics among the lay leaders of the congregation!

My swirling thoughts paused as I remembered Leonard's response, "there were so many other pressing issues so I decided to put it off until our next meeting. If we don't get the heating and air conditioning fixed immediately, we'll all freeze, and even fewer people will come to things. There's no rush to deal with the rabbi. I'm sure we can get her to agree to push off the date by which we're supposed to give her a decision."

"But we really shouldn't wait too long. And did the discussion about the boiler go the way you expected it to?" Lilith asked in a tone of voice that made it clear what she thought the only correct answer must be.

"No. I thought we'd be able to vote on a spending cap and pick from among the businesses suggested by the housing committee," he admitted. "It seemed pretty simple and straightforward to me. Figure out what we need and then determine who we can get it from at the lowest price."

"Yes, but I was surprised no one had talked to Elaine before the meeting. It's always nice to be able to support our own members and local businesses when we can, don't you agree?"

"Of course, but that isn't always possible," he replied without sharing the rest of the thought in his head, "especially when that member of the community is giving you the highest estimate of anyone around."

"But it seems such a shame to not even try to find a way to work with her," Lilith said, her voice dripping with reproach. "How else did you expect her husband and friends to react? It's understandable they would feel strongly that members of a community should help each other out when they can."

"I thought he would have more control over himself than that! It's a business decision, not personal," protested Leonard. Then he switched the subject again. "And if paying for a new heating and air conditioning system weren't enough, with the antisemitic threat we received last week, there's no way to avoid talking about safety and security."

I had heard enough. My mind was whirling and I could feel exhaustion creeping into my bones. I knew I better head home and get some sleep. I apologized to Detective Tara. I hadn't heard anything else that night.

Detective Tara looked sympathetic and understanding as he said, "thank you so much for such a detailed account. It was certainly much more coherent and thorough than what the kids had been able to explain to me. You've given me a lot to think about and follow up on based on that conversation you overheard. Is there anything else you remembered as you told me about all that?"

I wasn't sure it would help him with his investigation, but I told him about my conversation with Mina the next morning.

"Last night's board meeting sounded like a doozy," I said to Mina. "We heard all sorts of shouting and it even sounded like furniture was being pushed over. It really rattled the kids. And a couple of parents even stormed the class and pulled their children with them before the end of the session."

"What?!?" Mina was incredulous and completely taken by surprise. "I had no idea!"

"No one has called yet to complain or ask you to do something to mitigate the disaster?" I was surprised.

"No. Which is unusual if it was really as contentious and crazy as you say it was."

I told Mina, "I know some of what they were talking about because I overheard Lilith and Leonard as I was cleaning up. I'm not sure which of the topics set off the sounds the kids and I heard, but Lilith was clearly unhappy with how Leonard had conducted and handled the meeting. She seemed particularly peeved they didn't discuss my contract, so now my really bad feeling about that has grown. I know there are big financial concerns with the need for a new boiler and some upgraded security measures....I just wish I knew more about what was going on. No one will tell me anything other than the weird half-threats and bad vibes I got from Leonard. And based on what Lilith and Leonard said, I'm worried. And wondering if everyone thinks I'm doing such an awful job," I said resignedly, "you will tell me if you hear anything, won't you?"

Mina answered, "of course. And you shouldn't worry about the sounds you heard. I'm sure they had nothing to do with you. I know I'm talking out of turn, but I have to admit that does sound in his character, especially after how he's treated you!"

Mina's support was like a small ray of sunshine directed at my heart. I held my hand over my heart with a small smile on my lips then remarked, "thanks. I'm not entirely convinced I have the details about the boiler conversation right, but I do know it's a super big expectation to have, to think someone could get their company to donate a boiler or a whole heating system or whatever it is we need. I'm sure those aren't cheap. It's pretty presumptuous to expect Leonard to even ask Elaine to do that, let alone to assume things were handled poorly, or get angry about it!"

"He's always been presumptuous." Mina immediately looked horrified when she realized what she'd said. "I'm sorry! I shouldn't have said that!" she frowned.

"It's OK," I reassured her. I checked my office door was closed and leaned closer to Mina. "I'm not a big fan of his either. Just because he's a big donor, he's able to get away with throwing his weight around and pressure people into doing what he wants. But, you can't tell anyone I said that!"

"I won't!" she promised. "When you told me how he came into your office the other day without an appointment and just expected you to drop everything and have a meeting with him, I couldn't believe it! That's definitely the tactics of a bully. I couldn't believe how calm and composed you stayed."

"Thanks. I certainly didn't feel calm on the inside. And I'm really glad that now you know what he did, you're going to help be somewhat of a gatekeeper for me." I gave a weak smile. I still hadn't been able to wrap my head around what had happened the other day when I was ambushed like that. What sort of mind games had Leonard been playing, saying I might not have enough votes among the board to renew my contract? Did he expect me to run a re-election campaign of some sort? Or was he hoping I'd just curl up in a ball and give up.

As much as I felt like Mina was a great ally in dealing with this unanticipated workplace drama, I wasn't ready to fully share this swirl of thoughts and emotions with her. I took a big breath to steady myself.

"It's just not professional what he did. Next time I'll surely ask if he actually has an appointment with you and not let him just surprise you like that again." She started to stand, "and to do that, I should get back to my desk before anyone calls or drops by."

"I have work I need to do, too," I said. "But do let me know if you learn anything else about the board meeting commotion last night."

"Of course!" she said as she opened the door to my office and headed out.

I wondered if I should call Elaine, but just as quickly decided there was no need for me to intercede or get involved in the boiler issue right now. I would just try to talk to her after Ethan's Bar Mitzvah lesson later that afternoon, assuming she was the one who came to pick him up.

Chapter 14
Ethan's Lesson

My stomach made a gurgling noise. I hoped Detective Tara hadn't heard it, but I couldn't stop myself from stealing a glance at the clock. Whether it was my stomach or my eyes that gave my thoughts away, Detective Tara anticipated my thoughts.

"Rabbi Whyte, thanks for giving me so much of your time this morning," he said.

"Of course. I may not have liked Leonard either as a person or as synagogue president, but I never wanted him dead. I want to do whatever I can to help you catch this killer."

"Thank you."

"I'm not sure I'll ever feel completely safe on the Bima or alone in this building again until the killer is locked up. Even then, I suspect I'll still be jumping at every sound, and an old building like this makes plenty of creaks and other sounds."

"I also want you to be safe, and to feel comfortable again in your house of worship," said Detective Tara. "And I really do appreciate all of the insight and information you gave me." He flashed a small smile. "I still have a few more questions for you, but I think they can wait until after lunch."

"A short break and some food sounds wonderful," I said with a small sigh of relief. Then, taking a chance and nervous that I was in an ethical gray zone, I continued. "We have some leftovers from Friday night in the kitchen," I ventured.

"That would be lovely," he replied. "I promise not to ask you any questions about the case if you will agree to call me Misha."

"Misha?"

"That's my name. If we're going to have lunch together, I think we can drop some of the formalities, at least for now."

I hoped I wasn't blushing, as I felt a wave of gentle warmth at his words. "Then you should call me Shachar," I replied. "Deal?" I stuck out my hand so we could shake on it.

"Deal," he grinned as he grabbed my hand. He may have held it a beat longer than was necessary, but I wasn't sure. Clearly I would have to call my friend Rachel so she could help me try to figure out if I was reading too much into this.

We made our way down to the kitchen, fixed ourselves plates of leftovers, and chatted about things like our favorite music and other light topics while we ate. When we were done and the plates had been washed, we headed back to my office. Once we were settled back in our seats, Misha asked me what I knew about the Kleinmans and this whole boiler business.

"I don't know a lot," I confessed. "I don't get involved in discussions of building maintenance other than to bring the board's attention to things that need to be repaired."

"Even without being an expert or involved in the negotiations, I would really appreciate your insight into the family," he flashed me a grin.

I did the best I could and told him about my interactions with them following the big board fight. As I had anticipated, Ethan arrived for his Bar Mitzvah lesson wearing his soccer jersey covered in dirt and grass stains. I sent him to go wash up so at least his hands would be clean when he was touching holy books. I also opened my window a bit, hoping that would be sufficient to make things bearable during our session.

Ethan returned with freshly scrubbed face and hands. After bragging about what a great job he had done at that afternoon's practice, he was finally ready to turn his fierce determination to conquering the next bit of his Torah reading. I was surprised at how quickly the time went, and I nearly hit the ceiling when we heard a knock at the door I left propped open for air circulation.

"Oh my goodness! I'm sorry!" Elaine apologized, " I didn't mean to startle you!"

"It's OK," I reassured her. "I'm just a little bit jumpy after that loud fight at the board meeting the other day."

"Right. It was loud, wasn't it? Sorry."

"Ethan didn't tell you how spooked the class was?"

"No. But, usually the only thing he'll share with us has to do with soccer or some other sport."

I chuckled. "That does sound like Ethan."

"I'm still here, you know!" Ethan protested.

"I'm sorry," we chorused. "You're right, we shouldn't be talking about you when you're standing right here," I added.

"I want some water anyway," he grumbled, "followed by pizza!"

"Go get your water. We'll discuss the pizza in the car."

"Actually, Elaine, I was hoping you might be able to tell me what that fight was about. I know pretty much all of the items on the agenda had some potential to be divisive, but that seemed rather extreme!"

"I wish I could tell you, but we were actually in executive session for so much of the meeting, I think that part is confidential."

I sighed. "I understand. Thanks for letting me know."

Ethan returned with impatience written all over his face, and I locked up my office as Ethan left with his mother.

Chapter 15
Another Conversation with Lilith

"I know we've already talked about Lilith," I said, "but I should tell you about another one of the conversations I had with her in the days leading up to the murder."

"Please do. You never know what small detail might prove to be the key to solving the case," he replied amiably.

So I told Misha about what happened when I answered the phone the morning of the day of the class service and heard Lilith's voice. Rather than starting with twenty questions about that evening's service and ascertaining I was on top of all the details, Lilith surprised me by asking about Sam. She wanted to know his level of preparation for his Bar Mitzvah.

"Sam is progressing really well," I assured her, "but I think it makes sense to hold off any conversations about his Bar Mitzvah until after tonight's class service."

"Yes, of course, but I just wanted to know if his family has paid all of their dues and completed all of the Religious School and Bar Mitzvah paperwork," she said.

"I stay out of people's financial situations. I do my best to treat everyone equally and not be influenced by how much money they have." I said, trying not to let my annoyance leak into my voice.

"It's just that their family can be so hard to get hold of sometimes, and ..." Before she could finish I let her know in no uncertain terms no one was to disturb Sam's family about any of that tonight. "I am sorry to hear you have trouble reaching Sam's family," I said sweetly. "They reply to my calls and emails in a timely manner. And Shabbat really isn't the time to discuss business."

Lilith reluctantly agreed and more astonishingly, she even acceded to my request that she not drag Mina into the middle of this and to let me handle things next week." Before she could start asking about other students' or what was happening in terms of whole class meetings with the students and their families, I said the custodian was at my door with a question and I had to go. She tried to keep me on the phone, but I managed to politely hang up, and sent a silent message of thanks to the custodian, who was, of course, not actually at my door.

Chapter 16
A Friend Indeed

It had been a few days that felt more like a month, and I felt entirely wrung out by the time I got home after my day of telling Detective Tara every last detail I could dig out of my memory of the past couple of weeks. I hoped they'd be able to catch the killer soon and life could go back to just its normal level of craziness, because this was exhausting.

I flopped down on my couch and stared at the screen of my phone. I had a ton of missed calls from Rabbi Rachel Rubin, one of my best friends. They started on Saturday night and continued at irregular intervals throughout the day Sunday. I didn't usually screen calls from her, and would usually call back as soon as I could, or send her a quick text to let her know what I was doing and when I hoped to have a free moment. She did the same when I reached out to her. It really was unusual for either of us to have this many missed calls without sending some type of response. She was probably worried about me. I could practically see her alternating running her hands through her untamed curly brown hair and grabbing for something to nibble on while she paced. I wanted to pour out everything going on and my feelings. I knew talking with Rachel would help. But I felt too drained and tired to lift the phone and make the effort to place the call.

Maybe it was some sort of mental telepathy bond, my phone lit up with notification that Rabbi Rachel Rubin was calling, again. We'd met on the very first day of rabbinical school, when we were all smiling at each other with a mixture of nerves and excitement. She sat next to me at our first orientation session, and ever since we've been inseparable. We studied for tests together, helped each other to refine and express our thoughts, edited each other's papers, been there for each other through the ups and downs of romantic relationships, and consoled each other when rabbinical school challenged our beliefs and self-confidence. Although Rachel and I had taken positions in different states after ordination, we still spoke on the phone regularly.

I forced my tired muscles to respond before Rachel was sent to my voicemail.

"Rachel!" I gasped out as tears suddenly threatened to pour down my face. "I'm so sorry I haven't returned your calls. It's just..." my voice trailed off.

"I figured things must be crazy for you but I was getting worried, Shachar. Are you OK? Never mind. Stupid question. You don't sound OK. Talk to me, Shachar! I got your email about the congregation president, then couldn't get ahold of you!"

I had forgotten Rachel and I had subscribed to each other's congregations' email lists. I would open the ones she sent out when I needed ideas on how to phrase things to my community, and she would do the same with mine.

"Honestly, I don't even know where to start," I said as I maneuvered myself into a sitting position.

"Well...." she said, "your email said the president of your congregation was murdered. Was anyone else hurt?"

"No, no one else was hurt. At least I don't think so...."

"So it wasn't someone crazy who came in waving a gun during services or any of the other disaster scenarios they make us learn about in synagogue safety classes?"

"No, nothing like that. Those are all about how to save as many people as you can. There wasn't any sort of immediate threat like that."

Rachel let out a sigh of relief. Then I could hear the confusion seep into her voice, "but he was murdered in the synagogue?"

"I wish I could scrub my eyeballs and my brain out. It was awful! He was just lying there and I could have sworn I saw brains leaking onto the floor of the Bima."

"WHAT?!!?" Rachel shrieked and I found that talking with my best friend was helping to perk me up even better than a cup of coffee would have.

I told Rachel all about the class service and finding the body on the Bima. The words just kept pouring out of me, and the small sounds of encouragement she made coaxed more words to tumble out. For the first time since this whole ordeal started, my calm cracked and all the fear I'd been pushing down for the past few days rushed out.

"Whoa! That's a lot," Rachel said. "I'm not sure I can wrap my brain around all that and you've been living it! I wish I could be there to give you a big hug, your favorite tea, a cozy blanket, and a tub of ice cream."

"If only," I sighed a bit wistfully.

"I can't believe it was the kids who found him! And you somehow still managed to get them to lead Friday night services! If that doesn't make the board members or whoever recognize you for the superhero you are, then they are blind, crazy, and stupid!"

"Thanks," I said with a small glimmer of a smile. Rachel really did know how to have my back and cheer me up.

"Hold on a sec!" Rachel exclaimed. "The dead guy is the same one who threatened you and tried to bully you into resigning?"

"Yup. One and the same," I confirmed glumly.

"Calm down, Shachar. It's probably not that bad. You didn't kill him. The police will find the real killer, I'm sure."

"I sure hope so. Detective Tara seems pretty thorough. He talked to everyone who was there on Friday night, then spent hours with me to make sure he had all the details of what's been going on the past few weeks. Like the stuff I told you about that kid's Bar Mitzvah, and the boiler..."

"And your contract," Rachel queried. "You did tell the detective about that, right?"

"I told Detective Tara about that. Not telling him would make me look guilty and I didn't do it!"

"I know, honey," Rachel soothed, "you might vent to me or some other people, like that woman you take those walks with, but even then I have never even heard anything that sounded like a threat come out of your mouth. I refuse to believe you could murder anyone."

"Thanks, Rach. I hope Detective Tara can see that, too!"

"So enough with the bad stuff. Do I detect a little something in your voice every time you mention this detective's name? Is he young, cute, and single?"

"Rach!"

"Shachar!"

"Well ... he's not hard on the eyes..."

"His offer to let you sit in your chair so you'd be more comfortable says he's a caring guy under that uniform...."

"Stop it!" I said, sounding like I was about to initiate a pillow fight. "Maybe after the murderer is caught and put in jail...."

"I don't know... I think you need to stick close to the cute detective while he works on the case..." she giggled. "He sounds worth getting to know better..." I could picture her wink. "But seriously, I'm glad you told the detective what a bully your president was. Threatening you and telling a family their kid can't have a bar mitzvah? You can't be the only suspect! I bet the police see there are suspects who make more sense than you do."

We chatted a bit more and by the time I hung up, I felt relaxed enough to sleep.

Chapter 17
Back to Work

The next afternoon, I went to check on Mina before she left for the day. We hadn't had a chance to check in with each other since Friday night, which was only a few days but felt like a month. While she had handled things in a calm and professional manner at the time, I had a feeling she was not nearly as collected as the image she had projected. I didn't mean to startle her, but she seemed to jump a couple of feet in the air when I entered her office and said her name.

"Are you OK?" I asked. "I didn't mean to startle you...."

"Yes. No. I'm not sure," she babbled. "Is something wrong? Are the police back?"

"Take a breath. No, the police aren't here. I just wanted to check on you."

"Oh," she let out a sigh as her shoulders lowered a bit.

"You haven't spent the day fielding anxious calls, have you?"

"No, thank goodness! I wasn't sure what to expect this morning. I kept waiting for upset people to start screaming or fighting about security measures or blaming me."

"Why would anyone blame you? You were just doing your job. You did follow all of our safety procedures, right?"

"Of course!" she managed to sound both indignant and shaken at the same time.

"OK then, why would someone blame you? Unless you're saying someone has accused you of being the murderer?"

Her mismatched feather earrings swung wildly as she babbled "No! At least, I don't think so.... They don't, do they? Did someone say something to you?"

I knew Mina could get flustered and nervous, and like me, she was worried about the future of her employment here at SBM. I'd never seen her quite this rattled before.

"Let's think this through together, OK?" I didn't wait for a response to my rhetorical question. "If you were the murderer, and I'm not saying I think you are, no one who knows you would believe you would leave a murder victim to be discovered by the kids. You care about them too much to freak them out like that. I'd say if you were to murder someone, you'd be more likely to push someone into the water where they'd be eaten by fish or swept away or something." I gave a weak smile. I didn't really think she'd toss anyone into the river, but it was definitely more her style than bludgeoning someone on the Bima would be.

"Of course not!" "I'd never do that to the kids!" she sounded offended by the idea.

"So, why would people think you're responsible?" I'm sure my eyes reflected the puzzlement I was starting to feel.

"What if I'm the one who let the murderer in?" she wailed. "It's my job to watch the door until a greeter comes to take over. And there were so many people I let in who I don't really know!"

I was about to reassure Mina that everyone there was either related to one of the students, a board member, or a Friday night regular, when an image of the stranger sitting in the Sanctuary flashed into my mind.

"I can understand why you worry about being responsible for maybe letting in the murderer. But I know almost everyone who was there, and they're people you'd let in any time. Besides, letting the killer in isn't the same as actually being the killer. I got the impression there's a fairly good chance a member of the congregation killed Leonard. Maybe even someone who has his or her own key, like a board member." I could sense her starting to waver a bit. "If it was a board member, or someone like that, they'd just let themselves in and you wouldn't have been involved at all."

"But, what if it was someone who got in by pretending to be with the caterer?"

"Weren't the caterers the ones we use for practically every event? You probably know them all by sight, even the ones you might not have spoken with. And even if there was someone new with the caterers, I still don't think that would make it your fault. Worst case, if that is what happened, the security committee adds in even more steps before we let in people we don't immediately know or recognize. Which would be annoying and not particularly welcoming."

Taking a big, calming breath, Mina admitted "You're right. I did recognize all of the people with the caterer. And we haven't had any problems with them before." I was about to turn away when she exclaimed, "wait! You said you knew almost everyone who was there, not everyone. What if the person you didn't know was that guy who called the other day?"

"What guy? You mean "Jim Bob?!?!""

"Who is Jim Bob?"

"The antisemitic guy who called the other day. I've been calling him "Jim Bob" to myself for some reason. Makes me feel like our conversation was more coming from ignorance than being an actual threat."

"But I didn't mention it to the police," she whispered.

"What didn't you mention to the police?"

"That horrible phone call."

"Isn't that why they gave us their cards, though? So we could call them if we remembered something later? Call them up now, tell them about the phone call and our mystery service-goer. It's understandable it slipped your mind. But now I think we should tell them right away."

Unfortunately, talking to the police would have to wait just a little bit longer. Before she could lift the receiver to place a call, the phone rang. We both noticed the caller ID. I groaned inwardly. I should have known. In fact, when I stopped to think about it, I was surprised she hadn't called earlier. Mina and I eyed each other as it rang again.

"I'm heading over to my office in case it's me she's calling…"

Mina acknowledged my comment with a slight dip of her chin as she picked up the receiver and answered the call.

As I expected, Lilith was calling me to dissect all of the details of Friday night. If I'm honest, I was surprised she had waited this long to call me. Usually she took advantage of knowing both my cell phone number and my personal email to leave me multiple messages if I didn't respond to her within 30 seconds or so. Oddly, I hadn't heard from her at all either last night or this morning. A small part of me wanted to ask her about that, but wasn't sure how to do so tactfully, so I didn't.

Every conversation with Lilith was like a chess match, and she was an expert at capturing my pieces without giving any of her own away. I'm not sure if anyone in the congregation actually knew where she even lived. Yet, she extracted information from everyone else, and had perfected the skill of using your own words against you or getting people tangled up in each other's intrigues.

Today's conversation turned out to be no different. First, she wanted to discuss the message I'd sent out to the congregation. Honey dripped from her tongue as she told me I had hit the perfect balance between informing the community without revealing any details. I thanked her, but sensed there was something in my message she didn't like, even though I knew she would never come out and say so directly. I knew she was using this conversation as an attempt to get more inside information out of me, but I was not about to fall for that. As afraid as I sometimes was of the power Lilith wielded I was more worried about what the police might do if they thought I was impeding or undermining their investigation. Between not having my contract renewed and being sent to jail, the latter scared me a lot more.

Perhaps the events of the past few days had put me into a cynical or less-than-trusting mood. I was trying really hard to convince myself Lilith was just being her usual self and there was nothing malicious or underhanded about this conversation at all. But I couldn't shake the feeling there was more to the seemingly innocuous questions and comments. So, my feelings of being manipulated may have been exaggerated, but it felt like a calculated move to me that when she wasn't getting what she wanted from me by talking about the email I sent or getting me to reveal details about what I saw or heard on Friday night she shifted tactics.

I listened to her go on and on about what an important part of the community Leonard had been. She praised his work as a board member, and named a number of improvements to the synagogue he and his family had funded.

According to Lilith, Leonard was soft spoken and mild mannered. She lauded his directness and his willingness to engage in difficult conversations, as if she had not just recently had a very heated conversation with him following a board meeting.

After listening to Lilith go on about all of Leonard's virtues and her own inability to understand why anyone would want to hurt him for 10-15 minutes that felt like an hour, I finally figured out a way to interrupt her monologue. I asked her about the recent loud fight the students and I had overheard, omitting any mention of the conversation I overheard as I was cleaning up after class.

Her abrupt dismissiveness of the significance of the big fight sounded a bit suspicious to me. So I followed up trying to sound innocent as I asked her if she had shared the details of that fight with Leonard with the police. I wasn't sure if she was trying to convince me or herself as she talked herself into knots explaining why the events of that night couldn't possibly have anything to do with Leonard being murdered.

My head was spinning and I could feel the beginnings of a headache so I told Lilith I had to go. I hurried out of my office and practically ran to my car so I could go home for lunch and have a short break before having to face the rest of the day.

Chapter 18
Fresh Air

The next day, the sun was shining, showing off the trees as bursts of color. The temperatures were dropping a bit, and scents of autumn tickled my nose. I thought it would be a crime to spend a day like this inside. Since we were occasional walk buddies, it didn't surprise me Dani had the same idea. Unlike Leonard, Dani hadn't shown up unannounced expecting I would be free. She had called first. So when she showed up at Synagogue B'Kol Makom and invited me to join her on a walk, I was expecting her. When I saw her in the doorway, I grabbed a light jacket and jumped up to join her for a brisk walk around the neighborhood.

Since I couldn't spare more than 45 minutes, we didn't have enough time to go over to one of the many nature trails we enjoyed, but at this time of day, both streets and sidewalks were fairly empty, so it would still be a nice walk.

In some ways, talking with Dani was the opposite of a conversation with Lillith. Dani was not one for small talk, and she didn't beat around the bush. Sometimes her directness came off as a bit brusque, but it never felt intrusive because she was just as blunt and open about sharing her thoughts and experiences as she was about soliciting the same from you. It was therefore completely in character that after Dani complimented me on what a great job the kids had done with the service, we jumped right in to speaking about the murder. We compared notes on our conversations with Detective Tara and Dani shared with me a few nuggets of information she had gleaned talking to some of the board members and other congregants. It had been hard enough to know who to trust before, but now with Leonard's murder, it was even harder. However, because Dani and I had already shared a lot with each other on our walks, I decided to trust her with my suspicions. Since we were in a public place and not too far from the synagogue, I looked around to make sure we were alone before speaking.

"You know I'm not usually paranoid, right?" I asked.

"I've never considered you paranoid. When I was still working as a therapist, I saw paranoid, and that is not you. You are sensitive to moods around you, but you also always want to believe the best of people," she replied. "I've seen you do it, even when I worry you are being too nice. But I've told you that before. Truthfully, I'm not sure I trust too many people associated with this synagogue right now. Between what you told me about Leonard's impromptu meeting to drop a bombshell, the fights among the board members, and the weird tension surrounding contracts, there seem to be a lot of secrets and intrigue poisoning the community. But, where else am I going to go? It's not like there's another synagogue in town."

"I hear that," I concurred. "You know I haven't known who to trust for months, ever since I started picking up vibes my contract may not be renewed. Now there's been a murder things are on a whole different level!"

"I know what you mean. I've worried a lot about antisemitic violence in general, given the news we keep hearing from around the country and around the world. But the thought there could be a member of this community who is a murderer has me more scared than a threat of antisemitic vandalism or the theoretical possibility of violence."

"I'm with you there. It's really hard to think we might know a murderer. This doesn't feel like a random act of antisemitism to me."

"Why not? Mina told me there was a guy who called making antisemitic threats, and I noticed someone at services I didn't recognize. He left before the police got here."

"You don't even know if that person is the same as the antisemitic guy who called," I replied. "It could easily have been someone close to the family of one of the students. Or even a potential new congregant."

"If a potential new congregant, I'm pretty sure we must have scared him off and we'll never see him again."

I chuckled. "Showing up for Friday night services and being plunged into a murder investigation is definitely not a great introduction to a new synagogue!" Still, I hesitated. I really wanted to share my thoughts with someone, but I worried even voicing them aloud might somehow come to bite me in the rear. In the end, the difficulty of keeping everything inside propelled me forward. I leaned even closer and lowered my voice. "I had this thought," I practically whispered. "But, if I tell you, you really can't tell anyone else."

She promised.

"If I'm wrong and anyone finds out, then not only would that be the end of me being able to work here, it could get me blackballed all over the country."

"That sounds really serious! You sure you want to tell me?"

"If I don't tell someone, I might go crazy. But I can't go to the police with my suspicions. I don't have any evidence, just a really unsettled feeling in my gut."

"I've kept plenty of people's confidences before. You know I have your back. Am I correct in thinking you might know who the murderer is?" Dani asked.

I nodded. "I know you've told me to watch out for her before. I really thought she was on my side, but I wonder if it's Lilith. It was so weird how she went on about what a great guy Leonard was when everyone knew they often butted heads at board meetings."

"That's true. I did hear a few stray comments about that from some others."

"Plus, in her last call she was fishing for specifics. She asked a lot of questions about the murder weapon and if the police found it and took it for fingerprinting."

"That's interesting," Dani said almost breathlessly. "You really think she could have done it? I know I've told you to watch out for her and that I don't think she's always as nice and loyal as she tries to present herself, but that's a far cry from murder."

"Lilith and Leonard had been arguing a lot recently...and I've heard she goes to the gym and works on her upper body strength a few times a week....so maybe she could bash someone's head in...."

"So what do we do now? You said you didn't want to go to the police, but....isn't not telling them something also obstruction?"

"Who's going to pay attention to my bad gut feelings? I don't have any evidence. She didn't even say anything that was 100% self-incriminating. Maybe I am a bit scared of the consequences of being wrong..."

"Now you've shared your suspicions with me, I can keep an eye and an ear out. I'll let you know if there's more support for your theory. But, whether there is or not, I'm worried about your safety now. Promise me you'll stay safe?"

"I will certainly do my best," I assured her. "Thank you for listening and not treating me like I've gone completely off my rocker."

"Of course! You're not crazy. In fact, what you said makes a lot of sense," she said as we arrived back at the synagogue building.

We said our goodbyes and I grabbed a glass of water on my way back to my office. Conscientious of the fact I had just used one of the communal cups in the kitchenette between Mina's office and mine, I reached for the sponge to clean it. But there was no sponge sitting on the small sink, neither by the faucets nor in the sink itself. No sponge next to the bottle of liquid dish soap on the counter, either. Realizing that someone must have thrown the old sponge away, I leaned down to open the cabinet under the sink and grab a new one.

It turned out to be somewhat fortuitous that the door to the cabinet was stuck. If it hadn't been, I wouldn't have asked Mina to come help me, and I'd have had to deal with this latest discovery alone. We tugged at the cabinet door together, remarking on how unusual it was for it to be stuck like this. The "pop" when the door finally swung freely was almost enough to make us both fall back onto our tushes. But, before we started laughing at the absurdity of the spectacle we knew we must present to anyone who could see us now, Mina started shrieking and pointing.

The first thing I noticed was the candlestick. Even before I could finish forming the thought to wonder why it was there, I noticed there was something stuck to the end. Then I realized this same substance was what had made the cabinet hard to open in the first place. I froze, staring.

"Is that what I think it is?" I whispered. I'm not sure why I whispered, but it didn't feel right to speak any louder.

"It's a candlestick," said Mina, pointing out the obvious.

"Not just a candlestick. I think it's *THE candlestick*."

"*THE candlestick?*" As soon as she said the words, it was as if a light bulb illuminated over Mina's head. "You mean the one missing from the Bima?"

"The one that might have killed Leonard..." I said as we just stared at it.

"I think we need to call Detective Tara and let him know so he or someone from his team can come check it out," said Mina much more calmly and practically than I would have expected from her.

"I think you're right. I guess that means I'm not washing this cup right now in case that somehow disturbs the evidence.."

"That makes sense. You can always clean the cup later. But maybe take it to your office instead of leaving it here right now."

That sounded like a really good suggestion. I didn't need the police to somehow think my dirty cup was left there by the murderer. They would fingerprint it, find my prints, and assume I was the murderer!

We left the cabinet door open and Mina called the police. I headed to my office.

It came as no surprise I wasn't able to focus on work while waiting for the police to come and examine the candlestick. Instead, I kept wondering how and why the candlestick wound up in the cabinet in the kitchenette. Why hadn't the killer just dropped it after realizing Leonard was dead? Or disposed of it somewhere outside of the building. In books and TV shows, it seems murder weapons are always being thrown into dumpsters or bodies of water. The small creek near the synagogue might not be deep enough to conceal a weapon, but surely there were other places.

So why the kitchenette? Did it maybe have something to do with convenience? The killer didn't want to leave it at the scene but couldn't easily get it out of the building, either? It had to be something like that. I had barely come to this point in my speculations when Mina appeared at the door of my office with Detective Tara in tow.

"Here she is," Mina said and walked away. I invited Detective Tara to come and take a seat.

"Thank you for telling me about what happened this morning. Can you walk me through what happened and how you found this candlestick?"

"Of course," I replied. I wanted to be helpful. So, I proceeded to tell Detective Tara all about looking for a sponge and the stuck door to the cabinet.

"So, let me get a couple of things straight. First, you said it was unusual for that cabinet door to be so hard to open. How often do you usually go into that cabinet?"

"Not that often, actually. But I've never had any trouble with it before."

"And that's always where you expect to find extra sponges?"

"Yes, and dish soap. And paper towels."

"Is there anything else that's usually stored there?"

"Not that I can think of."

"Where do you normally store the candlesticks?"

"On the Bima..."

"Near where we found the body?"

"Yes. We also have some smaller sets stored elsewhere, but not any others that match that one."

"That one meaning the one on the Bima? Or the one in the cabinet?"

"Either. They are a pair. A unique pair different from other ones in the building."

"Aside from its location in the cabinet, did you notice anything else unusual about the candlestick?"

"Well, part of it was covered in something. I didn't touch it or anything, but it looked to me like it could have been blood. Maybe with some hair and other gore, too. Truthfully, I didn't want to look too closely."

"You did the right thing to leave it where it was and call us."

"It smelled pretty awful, too."

"I'm not surprised. Thank you for walking me through what you saw. Have you told anyone else about your discovery?"

"No. Well, Mina, but she was there with me, so it's not exactly like I told her."

"Perfect. Let's keep it that way, please. Don't tell anyone else about the candlestick. Not where you found it or its condition or anything. Got it?"

"Got it. I won't say a word. Especially if this will help you catch the killer!"

"Every clue helps! If you find anything else or think of anything that might be even the least bit relevant, please call me. I'll also instruct Mina to not mention this finding at all to anyone" he said as he handed me another business card, this time with an extra number handwritten on it.

Chapter 19
Kitah Kochavim Reconvenes

I wasn't sure what to expect from Kitah Kochavim the week after the discovery of Leonard's body. They could be freaked out, jazzed up, or have already put the murder completely out of their minds. With pre-teens it can be hard to predict. I'm not a therapist, but I do have a few tricks up my sleeve to help people process events in their lives through a Jewish lens, and I knew if there was any time to put them to good use, it was now. Knowing asking middle school students to share their personal thoughts and feelings almost never works, I decided to rely on what I know the best - our traditional texts. Using stories and conversations in the Torah and Talmud about how to deal with the discovery of a dead body would hopefully lead to a lively discussion and not blow up on me.

As the students came in, I asked them all to grab copies of the books we use to follow along with reading Torah. Once the students had a couple of minutes to chit chat then settle down, I asked them to open the books to Deuteronomy chapter 21 verse 1. Once a couple of students found it using the citation I provided they started calling out the page number.

Anticipating my next request, Emma raised her hand and said she would like to read. Happy she volunteered, I instructed everyone else to follow along. Emma read, "If, in the land the LORD your God is assigning you to possess, someone slain is found lying in the open, the identity of the slayer not being known, your elders and magistrates shall go out and measure the distances from the corpse to the nearby towns."

As Emma stopped speaking, the silence in the room was almost deafening. Based on the shifts in their eyes and postures, I could definitely see they were all remembering their own gruesome discovery. I gave them all a minute to process their thoughts before refocusing them on the verse and asking if someone could explain what this meant in their own words.

To my surprise, it was the soft-spoken Hannah who raised her hand tentatively. "I think this is talking about what to do if someone is murdered and you don't know who the killer is…"

"Kinda like here, but not," piped up Ethan. "This dead person is out in the middle of nowhere, not on our Bima!"

Sam's face was a sickly green again. "Don't remind me," he groaned.

"It also doesn't say if they know who the dead guy is or not," Emma interjected. "It seems an important piece of information when dealing with a murder," she said in an imperious manner that made it seem as if she was almost sneering at this verse.

"So what's with the measuring?" asked Isaac. "How will that help them solve the murder and find the killer? I agree with Emma. Knowing the victim seems more important than old guys measuring how far the corpse is from each town."

"That's a great question," I pointed out. "Do any of you have any ideas about why they are measuring?"

The class agreed that it made sense to measure from a dead body to a weapon or to other clues in the immediate area because that's how detectives on TV did it. They then specified it was done that way so the police could try to recreate, at least in their minds, what had happened. It helped them to figure out general characteristics of the killer. I was pleased with their thought process, but no one was able to figure out why anyone would measure to the nearest town. That was not a procedure they saw used on TV and they were dumbfounded when I told them this was not part of trying to find the actual murderer. It was about finding people to take care of the dead body and get rid of bad spiritual vibes.

"Don't they care about finding the murderer?" asked Hannah.

"Yes, of course they want to find and punish the murderer. But in Judaism, the more important mitzvah (commandment) is to bury the dead promptly, so that's what the Torah addresses first," I explained.

"They'll find the killer here though, right?" asked Ethan.

"Are you saying there is bad spiritual energy in the sanctuary?" worried Emma.

"Will we ever be able to use the sanctuary again?" fretted Hannah.

"I'm afraid they won't catch the killer. What if he comes after us next?" whispered Sam.

"Why would he do that? We didn't see what happened," scoffed Isaac.

"I think my brain is scarred," said Hannah softly.

"My eyes are," quipped Ethan.

Surprisingly, despite the outburst, they quieted down when I asked them to.

I reassured them in the case of our murder victim, the police were working hard to catch the killer, and I didn't think any of them were in danger. They were, however, a very bright group of students who may have seen or heard something that could help the police solve the murder. A part of me wanted to give them space for speculation, in case it would be helpful in jogging someone's memory or help any of them feel better. Fortunately my smarter side won out and we were not sucked into the black hole of wild speculation and increased stress and anxiety. Instead, we'd stick with what I had planned and we'd get through more of the texts I had prepared then I'd give them time for some controlled speculation.

"Read the next two verses silently to yourself," I prompted. "See if they help you to understand why they were measuring from the corpse to the nearby towns. Then we'll talk about it." I waited for the small gasps as understanding dawned.

"It was so they knew who was responsible for cleaning up the mess!" Emma exclaimed.

"Not exactly the most sensitive way of putting it, perhaps, but that's right," I said. It was the elders of whichever town was closest who had to handle the body and complete the associated rituals. Then they had to recite something." I selected a volunteer to read verses 6-8 out loud.

"And they shall make this declaration: "Our hands did not shed this blood, nor did our eyes see it done. Absolve, O LORD, Your people Israel whom You redeemed, and do not let guilt for the blood of the innocent remain among Your people Israel." And they will be absolved of bloodguilt. (Deuteronomy 21:6-8)."

"Did they think the elders were the murderers?" asked Sam. "It doesn't even say anything about evidence!"

"Good point," I agreed. "Some of the Rabbis of the Talmud had that exact same question. They explained what the elders were doing by saying these words was declaring the victim did not come to them asking for help, which they denied. They also didn't see the victim and then leave him alone to depart by himself without any protection."

"So, are you saying this thing the elders said was a way of denying any responsibility for his death even indirectly?" Isaac checked laconically.

Ethan almost leapt out of his seat as he asked, "But what if the head of the corpse was found in one place and his body was found in a different place?"

I think I surprised the whole class when I responded, "Great question!" to Ethan's rather gruesome scenario. "Our Sages thought about that too, but they didn't all agree with each other. Rabbi Eliezer said they should bring the head next to the body. Rabbi Akiva said they should bring the body next to the head."

"Gross! They had to move bloody body pieces and still couldn't find the actual killer?" Ethan was clearly fascinated and repulsed simultaneously.

Turning a bit green, Sam remarked, "there was a lot of blood here, too."

Murmurs of assent filled the room.

"I know there's lots of stuff the police won't tell us before they've caught whoever killed that guy, but do we even have any idea what happened?" asked Emma.

"And did the police clean up all that blood or is the Bima still bloody?" Asked Ethan, still focused on the question of gore.

Having looked in the Sanctuary earlier that afternoon, I could answer that one with confidence. "It's been cleaned up, and there are no visible traces of blood left. The police did cut out a section of the rug to take with them," I tried to sound as reassuring as I could. "It is strange to see the spot where the rug was cut, but as they said, that way they can run more tests on it if they need to without disturbing our Sanctuary any more than necessary."

"That seems very courteous," mused Emma.

"If cutting out a piece of rug is what it takes to catch a killer, it's all good," shrugged Isaac.

"Fine. But didn't the people in olden times care about finding the real killer?" demanded Ethan indignantly.

"They did," I assured the class. "Not everyone thought measuring how far the body was from the city was about a ritual performed by the elders. In fact, scholars in France and

Germany in the 12th-13th century seemed to think of it as a first step in opening the investigation. They thought measuring to the closest city would actually help them identify the victim, which is usually the first thing that needs to be done in a murder investigation."

"How does measuring the distance of the body from the city do that?" Hannah asked as a few others nodded long, signaling they had the same question.

"They believed the act of measuring draws attention from the surrounding cities, which results in regular citizens and relatives of the deceased becoming aware and being able to help identify the victim," I explained.

"They didn't have to do that here, though," said Sam. "When I was talking to that detective, it was clear he knew it was the president who had been murdered."

"You're right," I affirmed.

"And they had already identified the murder weapon," piped up Emma to my surprise as well as the surprise of about half the class.

"They did?" asked half the class in unison.

"Well, I figured that's why they asked me how many candlesticks I had seen. Then they didn't seem surprised when I asked about where the other candlestick had gone," Emma amended.

I hadn't really given much thought to the question of the murder weapon until I found the candlestick in the cabinet when I had gone to wash my cup. But it was clear from the conversation that ensued, these observant kids had noticed more than I had in that regard. They seemed to all agree that on the small table where we normally keep a big pair of ornate brass candlesticks, there had only been one. They vociferously disagreed with one another about whether this meant the other candlestick was the murder weapon. One person suggested it sounded too much like the game Clue while another thought candlesticks were often used as murder weapons. They probably would have continued arguing, but Emma took on a commanding tone as she said, "So, we know who was killed, where, and with what. Or at least, we think we know with what. But the question is who did the killing."

Normally, this is where I would stop a conversation like this one and remind the class about the prohibitions we have against gossip and talking about others behind their backs. But I could envision some pretty decent arguments about why that might not apply here. At least, it wouldn't apply if we were the police. Which we weren't. I reasoned, I could always share the teens' theories with the detectives if they seemed at all plausible or likely to help the investigation.

Having never found myself in a situation like this, I wasn't sure what to do. I hoped studying the text together would give them a chance to process the idea of murder without getting too much into the specifics of what had happened in our synagogue. I probably should have known better. Having the text to focus on did at least bring some structure and focus to their conversation for at least part of the class.

After multiple fruitless attempts to tie things back to the text, I realized the kids still needed more from me pastorally than what we'd done together so far. Since they didn't all go to the same school during the day, I belatedly realized this was really their only chance to process the shock of discovering a murder victim with other people who truly understood. So, in a potentially controversial move, rather than stop the conversation, I made the decision to let them try to make sense of Leonard's death for themselves. My role, I thought, was to help them have that conversation in the most productive way possible, and to highlight the Jewish customs and values, hopefully helping them find a little bit of healing. As it turns out, I was impressed with how resilient and thorough they were.

None of the students really had any sort of personal relationship or interactions with Leonard, but they were very invested in the question of who killed him. It was clear everyone wanted to figure out the murderer not just to solve a puzzle but to make that person face the consequences of his or her actions. So, at Hannah's suggestion, the students created a chart to keep track of their theories. They determined they needed to include: the name of the suspect, the suspect's relationship with the victim, motive, and opportunity. The police hadn't told us exactly when Leonard had been killed, but we knew it was sometime after I had checked the set-up for the service and before they got up to the Bima to lead the service.

I was impressed by the methodical way in which they were approaching this, but before they actually began filling out the chart they created, I stepped in to remind them it wasn't actually their job to catch the killer. That was the police's job. "I know this is important to you, and I think you have a nice chart here. But you need to be really careful about Lashon Ha-ra now."

"Wait a second," said Ethan with a slight furrow to his brow. "Lashon Ha-ra, that's like gossip, right? This isn't gossip! This is crime solving!"

"Lashon Ha-ra is more than just gossip. It's talking about someone behind their back," added Sam, "and not just bad stuff, either."

It made my heart warm to hear them explaining this important concept to each other. With the introduction of the concept of Lashon Ha-ra, the students got into an animated discussion about what it means to brainstorm and share ideas versus taking any sort of action, and at what point did that become Lashon Ha-ra? I was glad to hear Isaac point out that putting someone on the chart doesn't necessarily mean they think that person is a killer, so being put on the chart shouldn't impact that person's reputation. Sam pointed out that saying how someone was connected to Leonard also wasn't gossiping, it was just listing facts without any judgment at all. They wanted to be thorough, and I was proud of the fact they were working together to head off some of the arguments before they could even start.

"Do you think he was killed because of that big fight we heard?" asked Hannah.

"We should definitely put whoever was yelling on the list!" agreed Emma. "But who was it? All I know is the fight the grownups had was really loud and scary."

"I could put 'angry board person'," offered Hannah.

Before she finished writing, Ethan sheepishly spoke up. "I think that might have been my dad. He can be really loud, and I know he was really mad that night."

"Do you know why he was so mad?" asked Sam.

"I think it was because Leonard really didn't want to hire my mom's company to fix the heat or whatever," Ethan said. "He can be really protective of her. And it seems like the synagogue should use the businesses of members because that way they help each other." His words were greeted with some nodding of heads in agreement.

With that, the students had a nice start to their chart, and I realized I would feel proud to share their work with the police if asked to do so.

Suspect	Relationship to victim	motive	opportunity
Angry board person - Ethan's dad?	Board member	Something about the heat	

"If you want to talk about parents who were angry with the synagogue president then you have to add Sam's parents, too," said Ethan.

"Your mom is also on the board, right?" asked Emma.

Sam nodded, looking down at his shoes.

"Just because someone is on the board doesn't mean they have a motive or were angry with the president, I don't think," said Hannah somewhat tentatively.

"But maybe there was a reason she hated him enough to kill him and we just don't know it," said Isaac as he tried unsuccessfully to catch Sam's eye.

I knew both of Sam's parents were upset with Leonard, but I wasn't going to say anything right now. I wanted to respect Sam's privacy, and if he didn't want to say anything, then neither would I. I did, however, suggest the class leave Sam's parents on for now even if they didn't know how to fill out the row. I even went so far as to suggest they put all the families of their classmates on their list because we at least knew they were in the building at the time the body was found. Since they had already put two of them on their list, it was easy enough to convince them to add the rest, too.

Of course, my comment about who was in the building at the time they made their gruesome discovery had them adding the caterers, Mina, myself, and any of the other people who had come to the service to their list. They didn't all know the names of everyone who was there, but one of the students knew Lilith was "maybe on the board, involved in anything she can be, and definitely has something to do with the Religious School." I chuckled and said that seemed like a good description to me.

By the time there were only 5 minutes or so left in our class time, the students had created a fairly comprehensive list of possible suspects. Of course, they still had a lot of outstanding questions and blank spaces in their chart, which came as no surprise. I also suspected some of the students had information they weren't comfortable sharing in the group setting. So, before I offered to keep their chart safe for them, I also offered them the opportunity to each add to it when they came for their individual lessons if they wanted to.

I had to admit that even more impressive than the chart itself was the careful, respectful way in which they added to it without any character assassination or fighting amongst themselves. In case you are curious, the chart the students left in my care that evening looked something like this (the police have the original):

Suspect	Relationship to victim	motive	opportunity
Angry board person - Ethan's dad	Board member	Something about heat - Elaine's husband (the one who has the company...)	
Sam's dad (or mom or anyone in Sam's family)	Board member	Sam's Bar Mitzvah	
Caterer		Complaint about cost or the food?	
One of the students	Found the body		
Mina	Administrative assistant - works with everyone	Did they fight?	
Rabbi	Works with everyone	Maybe the Rabbi should fill this in herself	
Lilith	Maybe the board. seems involved in everything	Didn't agree about something important about the synagogue	

Chapter 20
Back to Normal?

When Sam came for his next Bar Mitzvah lesson, he seemed to have reverted to being an even bigger bundle of nerves than he had been before the class service. When neither casual conversation nor talk about his Torah portion calmed him down at all, I finally asked him point blank why he was more nervous than usual. I probably should have thought to start with that, because he actually answered right away rather than trying to dodge the question. He confessed to still being really freaked out about the murder and admitted to having had some nightmares about the body on the Bima.

I knew I wasn't a therapist and I couldn't magically erase those awful images from his mind. But, what I could do was bring Sam back into the Sanctuary and get him back up on the Bima. It was just like falling off a horse, I told myself. You have to get back up even if you're scared. I don't think Sam appreciated the analogy to falling off a horse, but he did follow me over to the Bima. His steps got slower and more hesitant the closer we got, but I kept encouraging him and reminding him of how brave I've seen him be. I tried to let him go at his own pace and not push him too hard.

We both let out breath we didn't know we were holding when we got to the top of the short flight of stairs that led to the Bima. As we rounded the reading table, I thought it looked like Sam had almost tripped over something, or maybe kicked something away. But, I didn't see anything, so I assumed it must be either my own nerves or something he did to calm his own. I had Sam run through a couple of the prayers with which I knew he was most confident. I was pleased to see a fraction of the tension in his shoulders relax.

When we got back to my office to go over what Sam should work on for the following week, I let him know how proud I was of him for getting back on the Bima. Sam sat silently for a minute, then with his head almost in his belly, he said in a voice so soft I barely caught it, "It's just... what if it was my dad?" he said timidly.

It took me half a second to realize what Sam was asking, and then I struggled a bit over how to respond. Gently, I checked to be sure I had understood correctly. "Sam, are you worried your dad is the one who killed Leonard?" He managed to both nod his head and bite his lip. "That has to be a really scary thought, Sam. I'm glad you feel safe sharing that worry with me. Have you shared it with anyone else?"

Sam looked stricken and barely choked out "no."

"That's OK," I reassured him. "I think it's a perfectly reasonable fear. But, that's all it is. Unless you know something you haven't shared with anyone else."

He shook his head. "It's just...he gets so angry...and what if...."

"What ifs work both ways, Sam. You can ask what if it was your dad, but I can just as easily ask you what if it wasn't. I know it has to be super hard, but we have to let the police do their job and follow the evidence. Until they've done that, any worrying you do will just keep swirling inside of you and making things harder for you."

"But...."

"When we don't know how to handle something, what do you think Judaism tells us to do?"

Sam shrugged and gave me a quizzical look. "Eat?" he ventured.

"Not what I was thinking, but yes, we do often turn to food for comfort and there is a stereotype of an older Jewish woman pushing food on all of her grandchildren and anyone else younger than her. But I was actually thinking about praying. Some people find comfort and familiarity in the words of the prayer book. Other people just need a space to hand over some of their worries and big feelings to God. And if it does turn out your dad was involved in Leonard's murder, then you have a whole bunch of people who will be here to help you get through it; your mom, me, your teachers, at least some of your classmates..." I tried to reassure him, but he wasn't convinced yet.

"They put him on the list," he mumbled to his shoes.

"You and your classmates put a lot of people on the list, Sam. That's part of brainstorming. I think you know that already. And if I remember correctly, someone made a big deal about putting someone on the list didn't necessarily mean anyone thought that person was a killer. It was just a way to see how Leonard was or wasn't connected to everyone. And your classmates are right; your dad did have a reason to be upset with Leonard because of the way Leonard was trying to block your Bar Mitzvah and was spreading some nasty Lashon Ha-ra about you and your family. But being angry at someone doesn't make someone a murderer. If it did, we'd all be killers! I'm sure you've been mad at people before and not murdered them."

"Yeah. But I did give someone a bloody nose once. And my dad is really strong. What if it was an accident?"

"That's a possibility I'm sure the police will have to consider. But your dad wasn't the only one fighting with Leonard. Lilith was too. And also some of the other board members."

"She was? They were?"

"Yes. There's a good reason your classmates were able to add so many names to that list. Sam, I know you're worried about your dad, and you and I both know sometimes he can be loud and scary, but in your heart of hearts do you really think he could have killed Leonard?"

"No. I don't think so. He was with us getting dressed at home, and my whole family came here together. And we weren't super early either. I think there were already people in the Sanctuary when we got here."

"Sounds to me like even if your dad had a possible motive, he didn't have any opportunity. You just gave him an alibi."

"I did, didn't I?!?" Sam brightened a bit, like a huge weight had just been lifted off his shoulders.

"Would you like to add that to the chart?" I offered. Sam readily accepted, and did so before leaving to rejoin his mother.

As was my habit, the next morning I stopped at Mina's desk on my way to my own office. She told me the police had more questions for her. Even though she was nervous, Mina knew she didn't have anything to hide, so she agreed to talk to them. But now, she was second-guessing herself and wondering if she should have called the synagogue's lawyer, Sherry Kahn. Even though Sherry was relatively new to town, having moved in just three years ago, she had quickly made herself an indispensable part of SBM by joining the board and becoming the synagogue's lawyer. I didn't know her particularly well, but I did know Dani thought highly of her, and everyone said not to be fooled by her small stature and propensity to show up places with a dot of food spilled somewhere on her wrinkled clothes. Her mind, I heard, was almost the complete opposite of her appearance. She was sharp, and won almost all of her cases.

With that in mind, I said, "Having Sherry Kahn by your side isn't a bad idea. I thought she dealt with business law, not criminal law. That's why she's helped out with contracts and building permits."

"But, the police wouldn't know that, would they? And this does affect the synagogue..." Mina's feather earrings brushed her rising shoulders.

"It doesn't hurt to give her a call to check, but don't be too upset if she says 'no.' I don't think it's the job of the synagogue's lawyer to work for or represent any of us individually, but rather to represent the synagogue as a whole. So, as far as I understand it, Sherry would get involved if, for example, someone from Leonard's family decided to sue the synagogue for not having adequate safety protocols in place."

"I hadn't even considered that possibility!" dread crept into Mina's voice.

Before her thoughts could become a runaway train going downhill without any brakes, I said calmly, "We can cross that bridge if we come to it. In the meantime, I think she's a good person to talk to. If you need a lawyer's help and she can't do it, I'm sure she has a friend she could recommend. But I am not 100% certain about how any of this works in real life, since the only other murder victims I've known have been in books or on TV.

Mina seemed relieved by my suggestion and asked me, "Do you know who the stranger who came to services was?"

"No, I don't. But I'm really glad you told the police both about the stranger and about Jim Bob."

She told me the police asked her all sorts of questions about the phone call. She even smiled a bit as she demonstrated how they had asked her to try to mimic the voice, even though they'd only said a few words to each other. I sure hoped I wouldn't have to try to mimic his voice! The police also asked for the security footage, but since neither of us knew how to retrieve it, Mina let me know the chair of the security committee would be coming in later. Hopefully he knew how to actually work the security equipment, not just use it like a window.

After telling me about her discussion with the police, I was a little surprised Mina didn't ask me if I had also told them about my conversation with Jim Bob and any observations I might have had about the stranger. Instead, Mina wanted to know how my class with Kitah Kochavim had gone that week. I told her all about it, including the chart the students had started of possible suspects. She asked if she could see it, so I went to my office to get a copy. I've read enough mysteries and seen enough murder shows on TV to know to always have multiple copies of something like this in case the murderer tried to destroy it.

I brought a copy of the chart over to Mina, and while we agreed this seemed a decently comprehensive list, we wondered what we might be able to do to start narrowing it down a bit. Both of us had unpleasant interactions with Sam's dad, but agreed none of our interactions with him had even a whiff of physical violence. Unless spittle flying in your face or eardrums threatening to rupture based on volume count as physical violence.

I shared Sam's assertion that even if his dad had wanted to kill Leonard, he hadn't had an opportunity. Mina agreed she hadn't seen him come by any time during the afternoon, and he arrived with his family once there were already other people heading toward the Sanctuary and starting to mingle, but he had a motive and we weren't sure if Sam giving his dad an alibi was enough to cross him off the list of suspects.

We spent longer than we probably should have trying to see if there were other suspects we could eliminate. It felt like we were somehow taking back control of our synagogue by doing this, even if it wasn't either of our jobs. Of course, as we went through all of the names, we took ourselves off the list of suspects while we were talking with each other. Privately, however, I acknowledged Mina had both motive and opportunity. Just because I couldn't see her as a murderer didn't mean she wasn't.

Sure, she was worried about her job, and Leonard was not an easy person to work with, but I had never seen her fly into a rage of any type, no matter how upset she was by something. I'd seen her bursting with frustration and worry, but I'd never seen her take it out physically even by kicking a trash can or slamming a door. I know she certainly had an opportunity to commit the murder because she has her own keys to the building and can come and go whenever she wants.

Plus, I presumed she had gotten there at least an hour before the service to double check things were set up properly. But none of that was enough to convince me of her possible guilt. For that matter, a lot of the same could be said about me. I also got there early to make sure we were all set, and I had my own set of keys. It was no secret Leonard and I did not see eye-to-eye lately. But, I hadn't gone into the Sanctuary. I had done that part of my set-up in the morning.

Neither Mina nor I had seen anything that pointed to the guilty party... My eyes suddenly went wide as I followed this train of thought. Mina must have seen a shift in my posture because she asked me what I had just realized. I told her I was thinking about how neither of us saw anything, but maybe one of us had heard something. At her quizzical look, I reminded her how sound sometimes carries in odd ways around the building. Some things, like being able to hear what someone says into the microphones in the Sanctuary even while being in the Social Hall, were deliberately set up that way. Other sounds, however, travel through the pipes and walls. I didn't remember hearing any noises while I was in the kitchen and Social Hall before the service, and by the time I was at the back of the Sanctuary, some of the congregants and family members were already beginning to trickle into the room. Mina, however, wrinkled her brow in concentration. She thought maybe she had heard something relevant, but couldn't put her finger on what it was. She promised she'd let me know when it came back to her, and if I thought it was important, she'd tell the police, too.

Gazing at the chart the kids created, Mina told me she learned something interesting about Lilith the other day. We both knew she was super stingy when it came to giving out any details about her own life and she almost always spoke and wrote in an overly-sweet tone I was coming to realize was a way of masking her true thoughts and feelings. We also both knew Lilith had a key to the building, and it was very likely she had been in the building sometime around the time of the murder. It was also logical to think she might have asked Leonard to meet her there to talk about something relating either to my class or to any other aspect of synagogue function. But it was hard to imagine Lilith getting physically violent. It's not that she was a particularly petite woman. Mina and I had both seen her carrying around large bags of supplies for synagogue events. I don't know how heavy the bags were, but I didn't think she was a weakling either.

Then Mina surprised me asking, "Did you know Lilith plays tennis and softball?"

"What?!?" I couldn't imagine Lilith running around getting sweaty playing a sport. I had never even seen her wear workout clothes! "Are you sure?" I asked.

"I heard her say so myself. She was on her phone in her car with the window down a little bit and when I walked past she was telling someone she would see them at softball that afternoon."

I was stunned. "Maybe she was planning to watch a softball game?"

"I don't think so. She said something about having both her racket and her bat with her in the trunk."

I was having trouble picturing it. Even though I thought Lilith and Dani were the same age, Lilith always seemed like she might snap if any of her hair was out of place, while Dani was happy in flannels and her wiry body was evidence the walk'n'talks and bike rides were not just idle talk. "Wow!" I said, still trying to digest this information. "If Lilith plays either of those sports regularly then it would probably be easy for her to pick something up and hit a person with it...."

"And she could certainly hit someone hard enough to cause some real damage..."

We both sat there thinking about this for a minute. I realized we had a suspect with opportunity, a motive, and maybe even the capacity to be the murderer. We might have continued to process these ideas together, but the phone rang and Mina had to answer, cutting short any further speculation.

A couple of hours later Mina burst into my office. Her breath came in raggedy gasps as she wheezed, "don't be such a bully!"

"What?!? What have I done?"

"Sorry. Not you. That's what I heard!"

"What are you talking about?"

"When we were talking earlier about how the sound in this building carries in weird ways. The sound I couldn't remember was someone saying 'don't be such a bully!' and then a thud."

"You definitely need to tell the police about this!" Had Mina actually heard Leonard being murdered?

Chapter 21
Another Call with Lilith

Since it was a day ending in "y" and there were still so many unanswered questions about Leonard's death, I was completely unsurprised when Mina told me Lilith was on the phone for me. I had a sneaking suspicion her main reason for calling was to pick my brain about the murder, but before she worked up to the murder, she asked me about all of the plans for our upcoming celebration of Sigd, a holiday preserved by the Ethiopian Jewish community. Since 2008, when Sigd was established as an Israeli national holiday, awareness of the holiday has spread through the world-wide Jewish community, and our community was using it as an opportunity to learn more about the Jewish community from Ethiopia. Lilith wouldn't move on to any other topic of conversation until she had wrung every minute detail she could out of me. It was not enough to share the various activities being planned for the different age groups, from toddlers through seniors both by themselves and together as one large community. Lilith wanted to know who would be leading each activity, who was shopping for which supplies, and even a minute-by-minute schedule. Once I had given her as many of the details as I was comfortable sharing at this point, I reassured her in at least seven different ways that I had everything under control for the holiday with the help of some volunteers and resources shared by fellow professionals.

We spent fifteen minutes discussing the upcoming teacher observations I would be conducting. Or perhaps it would be more accurate to say that I spent maybe three minutes sharing my plans and she spent the rest of the time talking in circles, repeating some of the salient details. I think she needed to convince herself that I was going about things in the best way possible. By the end of the fifteen minutes, she was talking as if some of my plans, which were informed by the latest thinking on best practices in education, were actually her idea and therefore, of course, both brilliant and the only way to do things.

If there were medals given out for patience with others, I liked to think I would have earned one for making it through what had to be at least half an hour before we got to what I thought was probably the reason for the call in the first place, Leonard's murder. I hoped Lilith didn't notice the more she probed, the more uncomfortable I became about sharing too much. Sometime during the conversation, I realized that I had decided I was not comfortable sharing my own theories about the murder. Even more so, I felt protective of the students in Kitah Kochavim and knew I would do everything I could to resist sharing the students' thoughts or the chart they had made.

So, before Lilith could ask me anything about how that week's class had gone, which I worried could lead to disapproval of how I chose to run the class or tense verbal swordplay to protect student privacy, I casually mentioned the police seemed to be doing a new round of interviews with a number of people. Thankfully, she took the bait and admitted Detective Tara had, indeed, called her with some follow-up questions. In true Lilith fashion, she didn't share any of what the police had asked her about. Nor did she comment on what she told them. Instead, she found at least seven or eight different ways of asking me whether I suspected Sam's father of being the murderer. She wanted to know if I had heard any of his fights with Leonard, and whether I thought he might have a temper. Lest I start to think he was her top suspect, Lilith was her own devil's advocate, managing to point out how reasonable he had seemed when she was the one to talk to him about Sam's upcoming Bar Mitzvah, and how nice it was to have his wife on the synagogue board. Since I had already taken him off of my suspect list, I was somewhat amused to hear how Lilith both proposed him as the chief suspect and then essentially talked herself out of believing him to be the murderer based on the few comments I added in response to her questions.

When I first started working with Lilith, I believed she spoke like this because she felt compelled to verbalize the process others might go through as part of an internal monologue. I also believed somehow this method tended to get her to not just agree with my ideas, but to become enthusiastic about them. Now, looking back on the conversation, I don't think Lilith ever actually suspected Sam's dad. She basically used him as a foil. She was not sharing her inner monologue or trying to pry out my thoughts so she could hitchhike on my ideas and claim them for herself. Instead, I was coming to realize, this style of conversation was one of the main weapons in Lilith's arsenal. Behind what sounded like a spiral, meandering thinking was actually an acute sharpness and effective subtle manipulation.

As she continued talking, it was hard to tell which of us Lilith was trying to accuse of murder. Having said all she was going to about Sam's father, Lilith next made a really big deal about the fact that Mina had let in someone unknown. What was the point of all of the safety protocols, she fumed, if unknown people were still let into the building. Even worse, this followed so closely on the heels of the antisemitic phone call. Why wasn't Mina being extra careful? And since the mystery man left before the police interviewed him, the idea this stranger may or may not have been the antisemite who had called the synagogue was even more frightening.

Lilith did not stop there. After raking Mina over the coals, Lilith began saying it was also all my fault Leonard was dead and we had police swarming the building and the whole congregation scared and in disarray. She never came right out and said any of that in so many words, but it was very, very strongly implied in both words and tone. The cynical part of me wondered if she was trying out different ways of pointing the police towards one of us while she literally figured out how to get away with murder.

I was very grateful when there was a knock on my office door that allowed me to gracefully get off of the phone and extricate myself from this increasingly uncomfortable conversation. Fortunately, it was just Mina poking her head in to let me know she was running out to the post office and not some new crisis rearing its head. After Mina left, I closed my eyes and took some deep breaths. When that didn't work to calm my racing thoughts and increasing anxiety that I was being framed for murder, I decided it was the perfect time to go check whether the supply closet needed any reorganizing or restocking. Focusing on a physical task would hopefully let me put aside thoughts of murder and guilt for at least a few minutes.

Chapter 22
Getting to Know Detective Tara

When Detective Tara called and said he had some more questions for me, I let him know I was happy to answer his questions or help in any way. A part of me, I'll admit, was also curious in getting to know this man a bit more. I hadn't yet figured out whether he and his family were Jews who had been hiding from the Soviet regime, or whether he was just curious and open to learning about different cultures and groups of people he came across in his work. I remembered that the plight of the Russian Jews had been a big issue when I was younger. I had recollections of people smuggling prayer books into Russia, and marches intended to help them be free to practice our religion. Before I could get too lost in my own thoughts about Soviet Jewry and speculations about Detective Tara's connection to Judaism, I forced myself to refocus on what Detective Tara was actually saying at the moment.

When I hung up the phone after confirming the arrangements, I gave the butterflies in my stomach a moment to settle down. I really appreciated that Detective Tara asked to hold this particular follow-up conversation with me in a neutral yet private space. It showed so much sensitivity! Since it sounded like we would be discussing sensitive internal synagogue matters, I balked at the thought of talking in my office, not knowing what sounds might travel through the pipes or who might be lurking outside my office door. But, I also hadn't relished the thought of having to go to the police station. I wasn't sure I could face the possibility of talking in one of their interrogation rooms, not knowing who might be watching or listening. Detective Tara's suggestion of meeting in one of the study rooms at the local public library seemed perfect! Unlike my office, it was private enough to not be overheard, yet it was both neutral and public enough to not start up the local gossip mill. An added bonus was the fact it would be dry on this gloomy, rainy day.

Approximately 30 minutes later, as we sat across from one another with some papers strewn on the surface between us, we both shifted nervously and cleared our throats at the same time. That small act broke the ice and eased the tension that had followed each of us into the room. I waited a beat then gestured for Detective Tara to speak first.

"Meeting like this is highly unusual, as I think you know. Especially since you are still a suspect." I wanted to object and interrupt, but he continued. "But, I'm going to go out on a limb here, because I need someone to help me understand some of the internal politics, roles, and ways the synagogue functions, and I think you might be the best person to do that."

"I'm flattered you trust me enough to ask for my help and that you were willing to meet with me in this off-beat location. I wasn't sure if I'd be able to really talk freely in my office. I was afraid we'd be interrupted by someone or someone might eavesdrop or something. And I've watched enough TV to know there's always at least one person you can't see who is watching and listening to people in an interrogation room at the police station."

"You aren't wrong. That's why it didn't take much for me to bend protocol a bit so we could talk more freely. I think I've been able to put some of the pieces together, but it would really help me if you could explain a bit about how some of the people I've been talking to fit into the organizational structure of the synagogue."

"I'll do my best. Leonard was the board president. The board is composed of a group of laypeople who are chosen by the members of the congregation. They are all volunteers. Each term is for 2 years, so every year half of the board is new and the other half has had some experience. There are supposed to be term limits, but there's no one who is actually in charge of enforcing that, so some people have been on the board for a long time."

"Was Leonard in his first or second year as president?"

"His first, but he'd held other positions on the board before. I know he served as a general board member, and I think he was in charge of a fundraising campaign at some point. It's likely he was on the board in one capacity or another for 10 years or more."

"What about the other board members?"

I may have held up my fingers as I listed them off one at a time. "There's Lilith Polshani, who is the chair of the education board. Sherry Kahn is Synagogue B'kol Makom's lawyer...Avital Rosenberg and Abner Kleinman are both board members with students in Kitah Kochavim. Avital is Sam's mom, and I think her husband, Dave, sometimes goes to the board meetings with her. Abner is Ethan's dad, and his wife, Elaine, is the one who has some type of heating/cooling company. In addition to Dani Chaco, we have a treasurer, but he's been away for a couple of weeks meeting his new grandbaby." I paused for a breath to let Detective Tara finish taking notes on what I had just said. Then he asked me to once again tell him what I could about the most recent board meeting. I repeated everything I could remember, feeling a bit like a broken record as Detective Tara asked me over and over about all of the details. It was slightly annoying, and a bit frustrating to keep repeating myself, but at least Detective Tara was gentle and kept telling me how helpful I was being.

I felt a little bit sick to my stomach talking about Sam's dad because I didn't want my own personal dislike of his behavior to boomerang and have a negative impact on Sam in any way. But I also knew I had to explain both Sam's mom's role on the board and his dad's contentious interactions with Leonard, including the fights about Sam's Bar Mitzvah. Detective Tara listened attentively. Then, to my surprise, I noticed a small smile on his face. Asking about it, my opinion of the detective went up at his recognition of how much I care about my congregants, and the students in particular.

Explaining the Kleinman family and their relationships and interactions with Leonard was slightly challenging. It felt like I was trying to describe a pretzel. I didn't think the Kleinmans had clashed with Leonard about Ethan's Bar Mitzvah. I did, however, think it was possible for Abner and Elaine to each have separate reasons to be upset with Leonard. Detective Tara said the police were aware of Abner's role on the board, but he asked for more clarification about how Elaine and Leonard clashed about her job. I was afraid going into the synagogue's boiler issues was about to put the man sitting across from me to sleep.

As soon as I mentioned Lilith's name, however, Detective Tara snapped back to full attention. I explained she oversaw the education committee and also seemed to be involved in almost everything else, too. She was on at least 5 different committees that I knew of, and who knows how many others she was either involved with herself or was informed about by other people. When he asked me to describe what it's like to work with her, I froze like a deer in headlights. At his reassurance that he would not share any of what I told him unless it proved to be important to the case, I blinked and words started tumbling out of me.

I told him things I would normally only share with Rachel, like how Lilith seems so kind and caring when you first meet her, but I'm starting to see how that might be just a facade. The thing is, Lilith's so generous with praise and overly expensive gifts that she manages to charm those around her. She is long winded, but at first that actually feels like she really wants to know you and how you think. Then, the longer you know her, the over-the-top gifts start to make you (OK, me) feel guilty for not reciprocating in a like manner. Then, they start to weigh you down like an albatross around your neck. I also told him how conversations with Lilith have a tendency to become more frustrating over time. The questions she asks about your personal life make you think she genuinely cares about you, and there's a part of you that wants to reciprocate that feeling while simultaneously feeling more and more uncomfortable in interactions with her. For some, like me, it takes a long time to see beyond the facade and realize she has extracted a lot of information from you while she remains carefully guarded behind a veil of discretion. When pressed for details about her own life, she manages to skillfully steer the conversation in another direction.

"Thank you so much for sharing all of that with me. I have a feeling you don't do that often," the detective remarked.

"I really try not to, actually. It both goes against my values and could really make things worse in my job," I said, unable to keep the worry out of my voice completely. "Sometimes I tell my best friend, Rachel Rubin, because she's the rabbi in a different town and I know she's a true friend."

"Your information is safe with me. I won't share it unless it's necessary for the case, and even then, I won't let anyone know you're the one who shared this with me, as long as I can help it."

"Thank you, Detective," I said while letting out a big sigh of relief.

"Misha," he said softly. I didn't trust myself. Was he asking me to call him by his first name now, when we were in a work situation, and not a casual one? I hoped the faint heat I felt wasn't my cheeks turning bright red. I was relieved when, after a barely noticeable pause, his voice returned to its regular volume and cadence as he prompted, "and what about Dani?"

I surprised myself a little when I found myself telling him all about how Dani has been trying to get me to see these things in Lilith for a while. Of course, I had to back up and explain while Dani is a board member, she's also had a lot of clashes with some of the other lay leaders. This naturally led to me talking about the challenges Dani experienced as a board member, and her descriptions of some of the dysfunction she thought ran rampant among the lay leaders. I told Detective Tara, (Misha, I silently corrected myself), that Dani and I often had intense conversations about how we handle big changes or challenges in life. We also shared thoughts about the future of the synagogue and Jewish education both in general and in this particular community. She was a sympathetic ear as my worries about my own place in the community began to grow. And yes, she had been at services that Friday night. She found a lot of meaning in attending services and loved it when the kids or teens were leading.

"Rabbi Whyte, thank you so much for all of this information. It's very helpful," said Misha.

"I'm glad I can do something useful to help," I said before adding, "and if you really want me to call you Misha, you should call me Shachar."

"Shachar," he said, as if testing out how my name felt on his tongue.

Feeling slightly emboldened, I found a way to continue our conversation a little longer. Then, Misha confirmed my fear that Lilith was trying to make me look guilty, even as he let me know he thought it might backfire on her. Fortunately for me, there were some small inconsistencies between the statements Lilith had given to the police and some of the other statements they had collected. Unfortunately, he wasn't at liberty to share any of the details with me. He was very sympathetic to the fact I now felt a bit unsafe at the synagogue. I already wasn't sure who I could trust, which was part of why we were having this conversation in the library. Since Leonard's murder, I've also felt uneasy in the building, particularly if I am alone. Misha expressed regret that he couldn't share anything that would lessen those fears, but he did offer to send a patrol car by the synagogue more frequently.

Chapter 23
Girl Talk

That night, I found myself restlessly pacing my apartment. My thoughts kept whirling around like the amusement park ride with the swings. I kept getting glimpses of legs and different color seats, but nothing was staying in place long enough for anything to make sense. My mind kept flashing between all of the different conversations I had had about the murder. I didn't know how the police kept straight all of the different pieces clearly enough to see the crucial details. Meanwhile, here I was wearing circles in my rug and staring at my phone without actually using it.

A sudden loud burst of noise had me practically jumping out of my skin. The sound came again, and my heart rate slowed marginally as I realized what had made that sound. I hoped the tremor in my voice wasn't too obvious when I answered the phone with a tentative "hello."

"Shachar!" the sharp, peppy voice practically leapt through the phone to my ear. "I've been thinking about you all day, girl! How are you holding up? Have they caught the killer yet?"

Relief flooded my veins. "Rachel! It's so good to hear your voice! I don't even care if the phone ringing nearly gave me a heart attack. To answer your question, no, they haven't caught the killer yet. So of course all sorts of things are still totally topsy-turvy." I filled her in on all of the developments since we had last talked, including what I had done with the students in Kitah Kochavim.

"You are so creative, Shachar!" she enthused. "The stuff you are doing with the kids sounds like the perfect way to handle things! Only you would come up with something so perfect!"

Her gushing put a smile back on my face, and it was with genuine love for my friend that I admitted, "I was a little worried, so I'm really glad to hear you think I handled it well."

"You know I have your back and think you are brilliant!"

"Let's just hope the parents and the board feel the same way. I haven't heard anything from them, which I have to admit makes me a bit nervous."

"I completely understand. But, If I should ever have to deal with something like this, God forbid, I'll have to channel all of your tricks and common sense because you seriously are a genius. Enough about your class, though. You seem to be leaving out a pretty big part of what's going on over there, aren't you?"

"What are you talking about? I just told you everything!"

"I don't think so! Didn't you have another conversation with the detective? What's his name? How did that go?"

"Yeah, I had another conversation with Detective Tara. So what?"

I could almost see her exaggerated suggestive wink. "I looked him up online, you know. Not bad looking...and he told you to use his first name?"

"Sigh. Yes."

"So?"

"So nothing. He's just being polite as he does his job."

"You keep telling yourself that. But I bet the handsome detective doesn't give out his first name to all of his suspects."

I wasn't sure how to respond to that, but then Rachel asked me what his first name actually was and I got even more embarrassed. When I replied, "Misha," she went off on a crazy flight of fancy that, as was predictable with Rachel, ended up with Misha and I falling in love and getting married.

"Oh! He can be your little Mishmish because he's as soft and sweet as an apricot and in Hebrew, Mishmish means apricot!" Rachel laughed. It was such an adorable thought and such a cute nickname I couldn't help but join in Rachel's merriment. "Now, go be a good little detective rabbi, call your Mishmish and tell him all about your new clues." She hung up before I could tell her I didn't have any new clues to share. I did realize the conversation with Rachel had pulled the corners of my mouth slightly skyward, and I had stopped pacing and was now ready to start settling down for the night.

Chapter 23
Board Business

By the time I got to my office the next morning, the giddy feeling of Rachel's gentle teasing was replaced by a knot of dread in my stomach. The board had called an emergency meeting for that evening and they made it clear they expected me to be there. A part of me was surprised they hadn't done so sooner, seeing as how they would need to elect a new president. Or was it that they needed to appoint a new president? I realized I should probably reread the synagogue and board bylaws. At least if I did that, I'd know what course of action was supposed to be taken. Whether that's what would actually happen was still anyone's guess. It was possible things would transition really smoothly and the vice president would become the president without any fanfare or squabbling. But knowing the makeup of current members of the board and remembering the awful fight I had heard last time, I was not too optimistic.

Either an appointment or an election had the potential for erupting into a disastrous situation.

I knew I could not ignore the board's request for my attendance, so I spent a while writing up a clear lesson plan for the evening, and put together all the materials the class would need. Then I spent an hour or so getting increasingly frustrated as I ran through a list of potential substitutes one after another with no success. Finally, I called Dani. Even though I was not looking forward to sitting through this meeting and would rather have been with the students of Kitah Kochavim, I was glad Dani was willing to step in as a sub for Kitah Kochavim for the evening. Unfortunately, that meant she wouldn't be at the meeting to act as a rational voice during whatever proceedings occurred. Though, I'm sure some of the board members would be glad she wasn't there to call them out on their poor behavior.

Dani wasn't one of my regular subs, but I'd seen her hold conversations with teens before, which is what prompted me to ask her in the first place. In my experience, I've found any group of teens can be either incredibly insightful and empathetic or completely mean, nasty, and uncooperative. Not everyone could turn the latter into the former, but I had a feeling Dani could. I was also leaving Dani with an extra detailed lesson plan, so there might even be some productive learning.

I wasn't too worried. At least, that's what I kept telling myself. Worrying about Dani taking over the class felt much more manageable than controlling my own fears of why the board members wanted me to attend this particular board meeting. Was I about to be blamed for Leonard being found dead on the Bima? Or for not finding him before the kids did? Or even for getting the police involved at all? Could it be they think I was the murderer? There were just so many ways this meeting could be used to attack me.

Once again, my head was spinning out of control. I was starting to second guess every single move I had made with regard to Leonard both while he was still alive and especially since he was found murdered. Fortunately, I remembered some of the calming techniques I had been working on with my therapist and realized now was precisely the right time to use them. After a few minutes of four-square breathing and focusing on the physical experience of the world just outside of my own body I still wasn't feeling particularly calm, but it was better than before...

Unable to put off the inevitable any longer, I headed to the room where the board typically met. As the board members arrived, they greeted one another and talked in low voices as they settled into seats around the large conference table. I tried not to let myself be overwhelmed by paranoia that they were all saying bad things about me, but was having trouble making small talk past the fear in my throat. So, it was almost a relief when Avital Rosenberg looked at the clock and commented the meeting really should start if it was going to finish on time.

"I agree. Some of us have to pick up our kids and can't stay late," remarked Abner Kleinman, Ethan's dad.

Looking around the room, Sherry Kahn asked "can we start without Lilith? Everyone else who we're expecting seems to be here."

Eyes darted all around the table as one by one the board members realized Lilith wasn't there.

"Where is Lilith anyway? She's usually one of the first ones here. Should I call her?" asked Avital.

"But what if she's driving? That would be dangerous," commented Abner. "I say we just get started and she joins us once she gets here."

Seeing some tepid nods around the table, Sherry rose to her feet saying, "OK I'll see if Mina left copies of the agenda in the closet with the pens and paper since I don't see them here on the table."

Time slowed down and the whole world went into slow motion as Sherry's hand reached the knob of the door. The sound of the creaking hinges seemed to go on for an hour. Inch by inch, Sherry opened the door and something began to fall onto her. At first, I thought it was a doll. Or a mannequin. Then as Avital shrieked, my brain kicked back into gear. That wasn't a doll that had knocked Sherry over. It was Lilith!

Abner rushed over and checked her pulse. His first aid training started to kick in automatically and he was about to flip Lilith onto her back to start chest compressions when someone else yelled at him to step back.

He obeyed and even put his hands into the air for some reason.

That's when a collective gasp went up from the group. Somehow it hadn't registered until then. There was a huge knife sticking out of Lilith's back.

I heard someone exclaim "Oh no! Not again!!"then Avital asked, "is she dead?"

Abner checked her pulse, hung his head, and nodded. Before panic could take hold, I calmly took charge. With a sense of Deja vu, I reminded everyone not to touch anything else and sent one of the board members to call the police and to wait at the door to let them in. I also requested everyone remain as calm as they could and keep their voices down so we could spare the students in Kitah Kochavim the trauma of seeing a second murder victim. A few eyes went wide when I said that, and people went back to their seats at the table.

"What do we do now?" asked Sherry, looking just as lost as she sounded.

I hoped it was obvious to everyone there would not be a board meeting that night after all. Instead, I talked about the custom of staying with a body and reciting psalms. There were some prayer books stacked in a corner of the room, so I passed them out to everyone and began leading them in saying some of the psalms in the prayerbook. I know it's more typical to pull out a book of psalms and work your way from psalm 1 to psalm 150, but we would make do with what we had.

I don't know how long we sat there saying psalms, but it can't have been too long because we had only gotten through seven of them before a familiar face appeared.

"What do you have for us this time, Rabbi Whyte?" asked Detective Tara, looking around the room. Before I could respond, it was clear he and his team had spotted Lilith's body lying on the floor. I knew it wouldn't be much longer before recognition kicked in and he realized it was the body of Lilith Polshani, the person who had been my top suspect in Leonard's murder. Unless there were two separate murderers lurking around Synagogue B'Kol Makom, I was back to being completely baffled about what was happening around me.

As the crime scene team approached Lilith's body, Detective Tara said, "for those of you who don't already know me, I'm Detective Tara. My team and I will need to talk to each of you tonight, but since it's late, we'll try to keep it brief, which means we'll be following up with you further in the next couple of days."

Raising his hand as if we were in class, Abner said, "there are kids in the building! The same ones who you already talked to when they found Leonard's body. You don't need to interrogate them again tonight, do you?"

"Thank you for letting us know they are also in the building. No, we don't need to talk to any of them tonight. We already have their contact information if we have any questions for them or if we think they might know something that could help us," Misha spoke gently. "We have no desire to interrogate or intimidate kids or anyone else, Mr. Kleinman."

I admired how swiftly Misha had diffused Abner's potential rage. Not that he was completely calm. He still sounded rather forceful when he demanded, "some of us have kids we need to pick up from class. Could we go first?"

Misha caught my eye briefly, and I could see the question in it. I shrugged slightly. With no reason why they couldn't accommodate that request, Detective Tara and his partner began asking everyone to account for their movements and started probing to see who might have a reason to want Lilith dead.

It was hard to wait my turn to speak to the police. I alternated between shock, disbelief, and uneasiness until, having asked for permission both from the police and from the members of the board, I opened up my laptop and began drafting the email that I would have to send to the congregation about this latest murder. If I thought the email about Leonard was hard to write, I found the one about Lilith even harder. When Leonard's body was discovered, I was the only one who suspected murder and had an idea about the cause of death. None of the students on the Bima with me had seen anything above mid-calf. I was glad they hadn't had to deal with the trauma of seeing his head all smashed in and I didn't let them know the goriness of the scene and I didn't share those details with anyone else except the police. I know the police had appreciated that, because Misha told me so. Since they hadn't yet caught Leonard's killer, not revealing the cause or method of death gave them something they could use in their conversations (or interrogations, if you prefer) with the various suspects.

While I could try to keep my email vague, I was sure not everyone who had seen Lilith fall out of the closet with a dagger in her back would have the same sense of discretion. I thought I might be stuck on a tightrope between what the police would want to see and what some of the board members might expect. I really didn't want to upset either group. The police could harass me, maybe even arrest me, and the board could fire me. That was a lot of pressure on one email, even if it was only in my own head.

I wrote a few words, then deleted them and began again. I did this a few times before I was able to settle on some appropriately delicate wording. Fortunately, I was able to complete a draft before it was my turn to talk with Detective Tara, so I could ask for his approval and get it sent before I left the building for the night. Here's what I came up with:

Subject: Tragic Loss

Dear Members of the Congregation,
It is with profound sadness and a
heavy heart that I come to you today

to share the devastating news of the passing of Lilith Polanski. Lilith's unexpected death has left our lay leadership and entire community in shock and mourning over this loss. Due to the nature of Lilith's passing, and the fact her body was discovered in the synagogue, both the security committee and the police have been called in to investigate. We know you will do your utmost to assist the security committee, the police, and one another as we navigate this challenging time.

Lilith was an esteemed member of our congregation and also a dedicated servant of our community, and her absence will be deeply felt. Details regarding a funeral and information about shiva will be sent as soon as they are available. In the meantime, please keep Lilith, her family, her friends, and our whole community in your thoughts and prayers.

Please rest assured we take the safety of every member of this congregation seriously, and we will get to the bottom of this and restore the security and sanctity of our building.

If you or anyone you know needs support or assistance during this time, please do not hesitate to reach out to me. I am here for you, and we will support each other through this shocking tragedy.

With deepest sympathy and heartfelt condolences...

I was grateful Detective Tara approved the email without me having to make changes. With that onerous task out of the way, I jumped right in, asking, "do you think Lilith and Leonard's deaths are connected?"

"It's too soon to tell for certain. We're really just starting to investigate what happened to Lilith."

"But two murders in one building? You can't think it's just a coincidence!"

"No, I don't really think it's a coincidence. But there are also a number of differences between the two victims that are immediately apparent."

"Is being bludgeoned with a candlestick really that different from being stabbed with a knife? Either way, the person ends up dead," I said, realizing how much this conversation sounded like it could have come straight out of the pages of the Talmud.

"Yes, and no," said Detective Tara. "They require different types of motions and strength, and most murderers who have killed multiple times have a preferred method they use. But I will grant you both Leonard and Lilith seem to have been attacked from behind."

"And they were involved in a lot of the same things in the congregation," I ventured.

"I know you already gave me an overview, but would you be willing to make me a more comprehensive list of things that involved both Leonard and Lilith?"

He gave me such an endearing smile there was absolutely no way I could refuse.

I smiled back at him somewhat shyly, agreed to do what I could to help, then added, "is here where I'm supposed to confess I had some tough or negative interactions with both of them?" I wasn't sure what I was doing. I didn't want to implicate myself. I knew I hadn't killed either of them. But, didn't the TV shows and books always say it looked better if the suspect confessed to things like possible motives as a way to show innocence and a desire to be helpful?

Fortunately, the man sitting across from me still had a twinkle in his eye and a relaxed posture. "It's OK, Rabbi Whyte. I already knew that." He shrugged.

"But I'm not a killer!" I started to protest. "Just because I was scared they weren't going to renew my contract, and we didn't see eye to eye on everything lately, there's no way I would have hurt either of them! I swear!"

"I know," he said softly and matter-of-factly. "If I thought you were a murderer, I wouldn't have asked for your help, Shachar."

I tried to stifle a yawn, knowing that we had a lot more to talk about if he really was going to let me help figure out what was going on in my congregation.

"Look, you're tired. It's been a really long day, probably for both of us. Why don't you send that email you showed me and you and I can talk tomorrow when we're both more rested."

"Really?!? That sounds good to me," I replied. "Thank you. I'm not sure how coherent I'd be right now."

He offered to stay with me while I sent the email. He then walked with me from the board room to my office so I could put the laptop away, check all the doors were locked, and verify Kitah Kochavim hadn't left the chapel in complete disarray. It was nice to have company as I did these things. I didn't want to admit that the idea of being in the building alone spooked me a bit. I spent more time in the synagogue than I did at home. But there was a difference to how the building felt when it was daytime, or where there were a bunch of other people there for a program. Now, our footsteps echoed in otherwise empty hallways and it was easy to imagine a killer lurking in the shadows. It was with sincerity that I thanked him for staying and even escorting me to my car, and we said goodnight to one another.

Chapter 25
We All Need Friends

When I woke up the next day, the sun was shining through my windows. I was glad I had already made arrangements for a legitimate reason to spend some time outdoors walking. Dani and I had planned to take a walk while she filled me in on how class had gone, and I shared salient points of the board meeting. Clearly, my evening had been full of surprises and I wasn't quite sure what I would say to Dani about it. In spite of all I had gone through, I was looking forward to hearing how Dani's experience with Kitah Kochavim had been. After exchanging greetings and deciding on a direction to walk, I decided to give myself a bit more time to think about what I felt comfortable sharing by jumping right in and asking Dani how things had gone with the class.

"You know I was already impressed by these kids. They really are a great group," she began. "And it's clear they all have a special connection to you. They were all so worried about you when they saw you weren't there for class."

"They are a really sweet, caring group. I hope you reassured them there was nothing to worry about and that I was fine."

"Of course. I told them there was another meeting you had to be at last night, and you were fine. You are still fine, right?"

"Yes, I'm fine. What were the kids so worried about?"

"Some of them were afraid you had been arrested and weren't there for class because you were in jail."

"What?!?"

"Don't worry. The rest of the class was quite adamant about the fact there was no way you could be the murderer."

"But" I sputtered, not quite knowing what to say.

"Even the ones who thought you were sitting in jail agreed that if you were, in fact, arrested and in jail, then the police must have made a mistake."

"How very reassuring," I said with my nose slightly wrinkled by my skepticism. Not wanting to give away the confidence Misha had shared with me about his belief in my innocence, I figured I should steer the conversation away from whatever people thought about my innocence or guilt. "They did, at least as of the previous class, have a lot to say about other potential suspects, too."

"I did have to stop some argument between the kids accusing each other's parents of murdering Leonard. I couldn't always follow what they were saying, but I think mostly they were all defending their own parents."

"That makes a lot of sense. I hope you were able to curtail the argument swiftly and move onto at least some of what I had planned for you to do with them."

"I did manage to do some of what you had given me. But it wasn't easy. First, the students debated whether Leonard's death was actually an accident and not murder. Someone suggested maybe the candlestick just happened to fall on his head, but the rest of the class clearly did not accept that as a possible explanation. Then they got each other spooked about some creepy guy who they didn't know who had been at the service."

"They aren't the only ones interested in finding out more about who that was and why he was there. Was he just a visitor who decided not to stay? A potential new congregant scared off by the discovery of a body? The antisemite who made those threats earlier in the week? It's always so hard to maintain the balance between being open and welcoming and keeping our community safe, especially when I didn't get any chance to talk to him at all. I'm not sure if anyone else did either. Did you?"

"No, I didn't get to talk to him either. When I first noticed him, I was going to welcome him and introduce myself, but in the confusion of moving into the Chapel, I forgot. When my eyes fell on him next, I told myself that I would greet him after services. As it turns out, I never actually got the chance because by then he was already gone. I didn't think he came across as particularly creepy myself, but I could see how an unidentified stranger at their class service could have spooked the kids. But eventually I managed to get the kids to at least do some of the lesson you had left for me."

I probed deeper to ascertain what, exactly, they had covered with Dani. Finally I could avoid it no longer. "And you, how are you doing?" Dani asked with a voice full of compassion and concern. "You have had a lot to deal with recently. That can't be easy."

"No, it's not easy, but I have to just keep doing what needs to get done. Even if my previous worries about not knowing who wants me gone have now morphed into even greater fears of being done away with permanently."

"Are you saying you think you could be a target? What makes you think that?"

"It's just hard to feel safe right now," I replied. "Finding Leonard's body was traumatic enough, but then last night..." I trailed off, not quite sure how to put what I was feeling into words.

We walked together in silence, each wrapped up in our own thoughts for a few moments. Then Dani, thinking she was changing the topic, asked about last night's board meeting.

"It must have been a pretty long agenda," she remarked. "It seems like things ran pretty late."

Either Dani was better at subtly fishing for information than I had thought, or she hadn't read the email I'd sent to the congregation. I chose to believe it was the latter because I did not think I could deal with any more scheming behind my back. "Actually," I admitted, "the meeting itself never really happened. There was no agenda. We didn't manage to talk about who would take Leonard's place as president or the boiler or anything else."

"That sounds fairly tame and positive, unlike the previous meeting. Unless this is your way of saying the whole meeting was about you..."she hesitated.

"No. That might have been better," I said. "You haven't checked your email yet today, have you?"

"No. Not yet. Why?"

"We had to deal with another dead body."

"What?!?!" Dani practically shrieked.

Fortunately for me, I was saved by the insistent ringing of my phone. When I glanced down and saw Detective Tara's name and number, I quickly excused myself, telling Dani I really had to take this. We had made it almost back to the entrance of Synagogue B'kol Makom, so I answered the call while hurrying back to my office, where I could shut the door for some privacy.

I made myself comfortable on my couch that evening and did what I had wanted to do since the night before, when it had been too late by the time I finally got home. Rachel picked up on the first ring as if she had been waiting for my call.

"What is going on with your congregation?!?!?" she shrieked into my ear.

"I really wish I knew," I sighed. "This was definitely not covered in rabbinical school."

Rachel let out a laugh. "Can you imagine? It would have been great to get some tips on how to deal with internal conflicts in general, but I'd call this class 'What to do when your board members are killing each other, literally.'"

It felt really good to laugh with Rachel. "It's just been so crazy here," I said.

"I'm here for you, babe."

"So, you saw the email I had to send last night, right? It was so awful! Finding Leonard lying there mostly underneath the reader's table was bad, but not really scary. I mean, the idea of someone being murdered in the place where I spend so much of my time is scary. But actually seeing his dead body wasn't."

"We do have a lot of experience with death. We've both been at a lot of bedsides of people dying, funerals, and visits with the bereaved.."

"True. I even spent some time helping out with the ritual washing we do between death and burial, so I'm not exactly a stranger to seeing dead bodies. But last night was different."

"How so?"

"It was like a cheesy horror film, but real. Somehow, even thinking about it, I see the same things happening at super-speed and in slow motion."

"OK. That does sound weird. But you haven't actually told me anything about what happened. All I got was your oh-so-carefully worded email that you sent to your congregation. Good job with that, by the way. I hate having to send out death notices even when it's a 95 year old who died peacefully."

"When I tell you, it's going to sound like I made this up. It's all just so surreal. When I replay the scene in my head, it's horrible, but when I try to put it into words... it sounds like a bad farce."

"OK. You know I'm taking this seriously. I'm really, really worried both for and about you."

Taking a deep breath, I explained all about the emergency board meeting and all of my worries about why the board members had insisted I be there for this particular meeting. When I got to the point of telling Rachel about how Lilith had fallen out of the closet with a knife in her back, she gasped.

"Now," I continued, "I'm much more worried than I was before."

"About your job or your life?" she quipped.

"Seriously. Think about it," I said, sidestepping Rachel's question. "I really thought that Lilith was the one who murdered Leonard. I think Misha even agreed."

"Did he now?" she said teasingly. "I bet your little Mishmish would agree with you just to make you happy."

"Haha. And he's not my Mishmish. He's not my anything. He's....he's... he's just someone who wants my help."

"Fine. We'll come back to this one when you are less freaked out." I marveled at how Rachel had just managed to back off without backing down. "You were saying you thought Lilith killed Leonard. But, unless there are two murderers running around your synagogue, heaven forbid, then someone else must be the killer."

"Exactly. And whether they were both killed by the same person or not, it means there is still a murderer out there. And I have no idea who might be the next target. Or how to protect myself. I mean, I thought that Lilith was the murderer because she was always so secretive and I overheard her fighting with Leonard. Plus she seemed to always manage to manipulate people and have things happen her way. And I don't think she and Leonard were working together on anything. On the contrary, it was no secret she and Leonard were at loggerheads over a few large issues affecting the congregation."

"OK I know that I only know these people from the stories you have told me. So don't freak out on me here," Rachel said. Of course, her telling me NOT to freak out meant internally, that's already what I was doing. "Based on what you've told me, there might be something Leonard and Lilith agreed on. Or at least, something other people might have thought they agreed on..."

"What do you mean? What is it you think they agreed on?"

"You," Rachel said flatly.

"Me?"

"Yes, you. From what you've told me, it sounded to me like they were working together to try to make sure your contract wasn't renewed."

"In that case, it sounds like I'd be the one with the biggest motive to kill them both! And I know for certain I didn't do it!"

"You don't have any time gaps in your memories?"

"Nope."

"No blank spaces? Anything you don't remember getting on your clothes? Anything like that?"

"No," I said wondering where she was going with these questions. Did she think I was the murderer? Was it possible my best friend didn't believe I was innocent? I was relieved to hear Rachel say, "good. That means it's highly unlikely you killed them while in an altered state or anything like that."

"Right. I'm not the murderer. I can't believe you'd doubt that for even a second."

"I didn't doubt that at all. I know you would never kill someone on purpose. But I saw this episode on TV once... But now we've eliminated any memory gaps or things like that, it makes your case that much stronger."

"OK If you say so," I was still a bit puzzled and couldn't quite follow her line of thinking.

"You didn't do it, even unconsciously. But, what if someone did it thinking they were helping or defending you?" Rachel asked.

"Wow. And here I thought talking to you was going to help me feel better. Now I don't know what to think. Are you saying you believe someone murdered two people because they thought it would help me in some way?!?! Do you know how messed up that sounds? Someone killed to protect me but in a way that makes me look like the prime suspect. Who would do something like that?!?!"

"When you put it that way, sure it sounds maybe a little far-fetched. But think about it. It could be I just solved the whole case for you. And as a bonus, I gave you even more reason to get away from that congregation and find yourself another job."

Chapter 26
A Dynamic Duo

After last night's conversation with Rachel, I was especially glad Detective Tara (Misha, I reminded myself) had agreed to meet with me outside on a park bench that overlooked the edge of a nearby lake. In contrast to the previous day's weather, the sun was shining and was neither too hot nor too cold. It was the perfect temperature to lure anyone to spend as much time outside as possible before the cold gray skies took over and we all had to bundle up in layers. I would have been bouncing off of the walls or crawling out of my skin if I had had to sit inside my office, a room at the police station, or even the room at the library. Besides, my paranoia had kicked into high gear, and I started to worry about listening devices or hidden cameras being planted in all sorts of spots in the synagogue. I even worried that something could be planted so our conversation in the quiet library would be heard by someone else.

Maybe I had watched too many crime shows or was exhausted by all of the tossing and turning I had done all night long, but Rachel's line of reasoning had really spooked me.

Sensing the tension and jumpiness I was exuding by the bucketful, Detective Tara approached the bench slowly, deliberately, and with just enough noise to alert me to his presence without triggering my fight or flight response. As he gingerly sat down at the opposite end of the bench, he commented.
"You seem particularly jumpy and wound up today, Rabbi Whyte. Would you mind telling me what happened since we saw each other last night?" He pulled out a notebook and pen and looked at me with an expectant expression. It did not escape my notice he had called me Rabbi Whyte, and not Shachar. Did that mean I had gone back to being a suspect? Or had he decided he was no longer interested in us getting to know one another better? Maybe he was upset with me for some reason. I just bounced my leg, not sure where to begin, and definitely not ready to share these new questions bouncing around my head. Fortunately, they must train police officers how to deal with frantic, distraught witnesses, because he remained an ocean of calm ready

to listen to what I had to say. After sitting silently for a moment with me still silent, he tried a slightly different approach. "Let me start again," he began. "Hello. I'm glad we were able to arrange to hold this meeting in such a beautiful place. I often find sitting by the waves and focusing on their sound and their motion helps me to calm down and pay attention to thoughts I didn't know were waiting for me."

That got my attention. It was such a beautiful description of the power of a place like this by the lake. "I don't like to meditate," I said, "but there is something sort of freeing about sitting by the water," I agreed.

He gave me an encouraging smile. "I wonder if I could get the captain to move the station over here so I could always work by the water."

My legs slowed down and I could feel some of the frantic energy ebbing away now as I couldn't help but grin at the image of a team of people and horses pulling the police station across streets and fields to bring it here. I didn't share this image out loud, but I said, "wouldn't that be something?!?!" I also felt emboldened enough that I was willing to try to calm at least some of the thoughts spiraling like pennies in a giant funnel, "And really, Shachar is fine."

"OK. But only if you remember to call me Misha. Do we have a deal?"

I nodded and shook his outstretched hand with my mock solemn expression mirrored on his face.

"Thanks," I sighed. "I'm sorry for being so... I don't know..." I trailed off.

"You seem really spooked and afraid this morning, and I haven't seen you like that before," remarked Misha with words undergirded by real concern and compassion. "I keep forgetting how awful this must be for you. I'm used to seeing dead bodies, and sometimes forget how others might be reacting."

"It's not the dead bodies," I jumped in. "I'm OK with dead bodies. I sit with people who are dying, and help prepare bodies for funerals. It's the murder part I'm not OK with. Not that anyone should be OK with murder, but..."

Despite me feeling completely incoherent, Misha seemed to be following what I was trying to say. "Is it the gore that tends to accompany murder that bothers you so much, or the fact that there is a murderer at all?"

"Definitely the latter. When it was just Leonard it wasn't so bad. He rubbed a lot of people the wrong way. So, I could tell myself he was the target for a reason."

"That makes a lot of sense. But it's not how you feel now?"

"No. I mean, the same could be said about Lilith. She was like a force of nature who knocked over people who didn't fit with her vision. But she did it with a sweet voice and piles of presents, so it could be harder to get a handle on why someone would kill her. But she stirred up lots of emotions in people, so, if it were just Lilith who'd been killed, I think I would still be able to handle it...."

"But since it's both Leonard and Lilith...." Misha trailed off, clearly hoping I would jump in to finish the thought.

I waited a bit, trying to put words to my thoughts. "It makes me worry there might be more people this person intends to kill. But I can't figure out who they might be, which makes it more scary," I confessed.

"I won't lie to you. That is a possibility. But this doesn't feel like either a rampage or a typical serial killer. The locations of the bodies and the methods used seem quite deliberate. I believe the killer has a list of specific targets, but right now, I couldn't say whether there are others on that list or not. Since you spend so much time in the building where both of these murders occurred, promise me you'll be careful until we catch this murderer, Shachar."

"I'm trying. But it's hard to know exactly what that entails. I can't not go to work, but I also worry someone is lurking around the building. It's part of the reason I'm glad we are having this conversation out here in the open. Both Leonard and Lilith were found inside the synagogue. And their bodies were both left in pretty small spaces. So, here we are in a big open space, the opposite of where they were found."

"That's pretty good reasoning, there," Misha conceded. "But we both know weather like this can't be counted on. Plus I think we both want to capture this killer as soon as possible, right?" He seemed to be leading up to something, and I wasn't sure I was going to like it. "So, be honest with me, Shachar, what really has you spooked this morning?"

I took a deep breath in an attempt to steady nerves that threatened to explode again. "Two things, really," I confessed. "I know you are the detective, and it's not really my job to catch the murderer. But, I had myself convinced I knew who killed Leonard. I thought all we needed was a little bit more concrete evidence. Now, I don't trust my own reasoning or my own impressions of the people with whom I spend so much time."

"Are you saying what I think you're saying? You thought Lilith was Leonard's murderer."

I nodded. "Exactly. Maybe it was just wishful thinking because I had been having difficulty communicating with both of them. I didn't hate either of them or anything, though. I just felt hurt by both of them. And I was really worried about my job. Actually, I still am. I was almost certain it was Lilith who had killed Leonard based on what I know of their interactions lately. But if Lilith killed Leonard, there is still the question of who killed Lilith, which makes me feel like I'm back at square one and jumping at the sight of a shadow. And it seems maybe a little crazy, but I don't know if I'm more scared I might be a target of a murderer or of a group of people who want to fire me from my job."

"If I were you, right now I'd worry more about the murderer. You can get another job if you need to, but you can't just get a new life."

"When you put it way...."

"I'm not trying to make you more afraid."

"I know, but..."

"Maybe you need to talk to someone. I can give you the name of the person the department usually recommends victims or witnesses talk to if they are having a rough time", Misha offered.

"Thanks. I'll think about it. I do have another outlet, though. I thought talking to my best friend Rachel would help. But we talked last night and that just made me feel worse," I buried my face in my hands. I could sense that Misha wanted to comfort me, but he felt constrained to maintain official boundaries.

"What did your friend say that got you so upset?" he asked softly.

Still not meeting Misha's eyes, I managed to say, "we were talking about who might have a reason to want to kill both Leonard and Lilith. Then we realized by that line of reasoning, there are some people who will think that makes me the most likely suspect. But I know it wasn't me. Then Rachel brought up the possibility someone wanted to frame me for these murders. So, Rachel started asking if I might have a stalker or someone who hates me enough to want to frame me. So now I'm worried about having a stalker!"

"Your instinct to try to think of one person who might have wanted to kill both of them is also what I am following up on today. Have you noticed anyone who has been following you around?"

"Not that I can really think of," I said with my shoulders rising.

"What about a feeling of being watched? Or someone who seems to know more about what's happening in your life than you would expect them to?"

"I don't know," I practically wailed then took a deep breath. "I'm sorry. I'm not usually this outwardly an emotional mess."

"No need to apologize. I know that these are really tough things to even think about, let alone experience. The good news is that based on what you just said, I don't think you have a stalker. Unfortunately, that doesn't rule out someone trying to frame you. Would you be OK if we tried to approach this from a slightly different angle? We're going to set aside the question of motive and instead focus on opportunity."

"OK. I can try," I said in a smaller voice I tried to project.

"First, I'd like you to help me make lists of who was in the building each of those two nights."

That I had no problem doing. Misha ripped two pages out of his notebook, and labeled them "Leonard" and "Lilith" respectively. Together, we generated lists of everyone we could think of who had been in the building each of those two days for up to two hours before the bodies had been found. Misha told me that was the time frame the coroner had suggested for time of death in both cases.

"Great. I think it makes the most sense to start with the theory we are dealing with one murderer in your congregation. I think that's what everyone is hoping. And it seems most likely, even though they were killed in different ways," Misha said.

It sounded like a good idea to me, so together we went through the list highlighting who had been there both times. There was a rather large overlap, as I knew there would be. We were, however, able to set aside the possibility of the unknown service attendee, whether he was "Jim Bob" or not, and anyone associated with the caterer, since none of them had been there at all on the day when Lilith's body was discovered.

Misha asked if I could help him with one last thing. He was afraid asking would make me upset again, but we both recognized I was really the best person to tackle this. He wanted me to go through the list of the names of the people we had highlighted and to just write down a few words about the types of interactions I had with them. I agreed. Rather than upsetting me, having this task to do made me feel as if I was back in control, at least to some degree.

I decided there was no time like the present, and this felt much more urgent than anything waiting for me back in my office. Plus, taking care of it now let me enjoy the nice weather and the view a little bit longer. I decided to start with the students in Kitah Kochavim because I thought that would be the easiest and most straightforward. I started by matching children with their parents, and putting an asterisk next to the names of the parents who were board members. Then, I added in notes about the connections members of a given family had with Leonard, Lilith, or both.

When I explained my notes to Misha, he agreed with me that Emma Silverman, Hannah Berman, Isaac Weiss, and their family members had little to no direct contact with Leonard, and only minimal contact with Lilith through her work with the Religious School. Their parents were not on the board, and they were not facing any issues with 'Bar/Bat' mitzvah preparation. It's possible some of them may still have owed some or all of their tuition or membership dues. But, neither Leonard nor Lilith was the treasurer... Not that it stopped either of them from trying to do work that rightly fell under someone else's purview.

Ethan Kleinman and his parents, Elaine and Abner, however, did have a reason why they might be upset with Leonard. Even though it wasn't just Leonard who had voted not to use Elaine's company to work on the synagogue's heating and cooling systems, it's easy to see how one might lay the blame for the decision on the president. Especially when said president had a reputation of throwing his weight around. Any one of the three of them might have been angry enough with Leonard to hit him with the nearest thing at hand if he'd been saying bad things about Elaine's company. He may even have had enough clout with enough people to bring about the Kleinman's financial ruin. But I didn't know of any issues any of them might have had against Lilith. Though, given Abner was on the board with her, it is always possible they had more animosity toward one another than I knew. I don't think any of them felt strongly enough about me for that to be a factor for any of them. I did, however, encourage Misha to follow up with them more in case I had missed something.

The only other student who had a parent on the board was Sam Rosenberg. The Rosenbergs had extensive interactions with both Leonard and Lilith in regard to Sam's upcoming Bar Mitzvah, among other things. Lifecycle events have been known to occasionally bring out the crazy in people. There are the Bridezillas and the Demanding Moms, and parents and grandparents from each side of the family trying to outdo each other. And the negotiations involved in planning a Bar Mitzvah when the parents had an acrimonious divorce can get complicated. I couldn't be 100% positive, but I thought that everyone in the family got along with Lilith. Still, if he thought it had even the slightest possibility of helping find the murderer, I would back Misha up with no hesitation if he wanted to talk to any of them again.

Having worked my way through the students of Kitah Kochavim and their family members, I turned my attention to any other board members who had also been in the building during the few hours leading up to and including the service led by Kitah Kochavim. I realized there were only two of them, Sherry Kahn and Dani Chaco. I didn't really know Sherry very well. We had made small talk before or after services, but I'd never had any interactions with her that gave me any insight into her relationships with either Leonard or Lilith. I didn't think she had extreme emotions about me, but who knows. She had never come to complain to me or give me any negative feedback that would lead me to think she would have any reason to want to frame me. Though, I did recall one episode of a TV crime show where the killer framed someone because it was convenient, not because of how they felt about the person they framed. So I supposed that was a possibility, even if it seemed rather unlikely. I also couldn't wrap my head around the idea Sherry could have either cared so much about me or known about my difficulties with Leonard and Lilith to have gone so far as to kill either of them. She hadn't acted like a stalker or anything.

This brought me to Dani. I knew Dani wasn't a fan of either Leonard or Lilith. I had heard her complain about both of them extensively on our "walk'n'talks." But I'd never known her to be violent or anything like that. Sure, she was stronger than a lot of other women her age because she did a lot of walking and biking, nothing to strengthen her arms or upper body. Besides, I thought she was dealing with her frustration at their inefficiency and controlling natures by simply stepping down from the board so she wouldn't have to interact with either of them.

As hard as it was for me to picture Dani as the murderer, it seemed at least 100 times more likely than suspecting Mina. Yes, I know on TV and in books it's not unheard of for the quiet, meek, overlooked person to be unmasked as the murderer. Then we learn about all of this resentment, anger, and bundle of other negative emotions they have been swallowing until the point where they can't hold it in any longer and they burst. But, Mina hadn't been holding her feelings in around me. We had talked about the aspects of our respective jobs and the people in the congregation who tended to make it harder for us to do our jobs for one reason or another. I know she had differences of opinion with both Leonard and Lilith, and she interacted with both of them on a regular basis, but I had a really hard time picturing her murdering anyone, much less doing so in the space where she worked and spent so much of her time. But, I trusted the police to do a thorough investigation.

I didn't know how helpful any of these notes would be, but I shared them with Misha anyway. Maybe he'd see something in my musings I hadn't. He did have the benefit of more emotional distance than I did, after all.

Chapter 27
Panic Rising

When I walked in the Synagogue after my meeting with Misha, Mina practically leapt out of her seat and pounced on me.

"Are you OK?" she asked.

"I'm fine," I answered.

"Really?!? You weren't here, which is not like you, so I got really worried. I'm so glad to see you are alive and not in the hospital or jail or anything."

"I really didn't mean to worry you. I had a meeting out of the building and it went longer than I had expected, that's all."

"So you're sure you really are OK? Because it would make sense if you're not, you know. I was going to call in sick or work from home. I'm really nervous being here. But I can't afford to lose this job right now. How can they expect us to come into work like everything is normal when you've found two dead bodies!"

"What else are we supposed to do?" I asked. "We both have responsibilities here, and they aren't all things we can handle remotely. But we can try not to be alone..."

"You're right. I'm just worried and wonder if we shouldn't just cancel everything until the police find the murderer."

"While I will admit that idea has a certain appeal, and might make some people feel safer, it also sends the message we shouldn't trust each other. That's certainly not what I want members of this community to think or feel. Obviously if the police, the security committee, or the board members who are left tell us to close, we will. But we need to hold space for our community to continue to gather to support one another even if they are afraid. In the meantime, you can help me and probably everyone else, too by doing what you do best. You can answer the phones and not put any reporters or frantic congregants through to me."

"What should I say to them?'

"As far as the reporters go, 'no comment' generally seems to work. As for congregants, I can imagine a few different scenarios."

"Let me get a pen and paper to make sure I get this right."

"Ready?" I waited for her nod before continuing, "anyone who wants to know any details of the case or specifics should be referred to the police. For those worried about the security of the building, you should remind them we take security very seriously, and the police are not convinced there was any breach of security that allowed a killer into the building. For inquiries about classes, services, or the building being open in general, say we're doing our best to continue normal operations and will communicate any changes via email and on our website."

"Got it. Thank you. You put things so nicely and clearly. Case details - call the police. Security - not sure there was a breach of security. Classes and meetings - yes unless you hear otherwise. I think you're right these will help calm people down. Though, I don't think that means you'll see them coming through those doors anytime soon."

"Maybe not. But it's worth a shot. And if the bit about security doesn't help, then feel free to refer the caller to either the head of our security committee or to the police."

"Thanks. I think this might just keep me sane for the day."

"You're welcome," I said. I wasn't sure I had actually done anything, but Mina felt better. Even better, from my perspective, I had managed to do so without signing myself up to handle any extra work.

As I was about to head to my own office, Mina called out, "wait! I have a question." I stopped in my tracks and waited while Mina figured out how to ask me her question. "When you said you didn't think there had been any breach of security, what did you mean? There have been two people killed in our building! How is that not a security breach?"

"The focus of our security measures is about getting into the building. Not about what happens inside. We have cameras that show us what is outside each of the doors one might use to come in, and we have greeters and lists of names to monitor who is entering. But, the only real security measures we have inside the building are some office and classroom doors that lock, and plans for where to go if we need to evacuate."

"I never thought about that!" Mina exclaimed. "We're worried about antisemitic shooters and bombs, but until now, it never even crossed my mind the people who pose the most danger could be ones who have keys to the building and can walk in whenever they please!" She shivered. "I think that might be worse!"

"Yup. The thought it's someone we know and trust who has committed these murders is terrifying. But it's also reassuring in a way."

"How could it even possibly be reassuring?"

"If the killer has specific reasons for selecting these particular victims, then the majority of us are safe. The kids especially."

"I hear what you're saying, but I'm still not reassured. Though, being able to tell parents we don't think the kids are in any danger is definitely a good thing."

Even with all of the reassurances I gave Mina, I was not surprised the remaining board members decided to hold their second attempt at an emergency meeting virtually. I admit I was somewhat relieved that even with the ability to attend the meeting from my own couch instead of the board room, the remaining board members hadn't insisted on me attending. As much as I kept telling Mina and Rachel that I was fine, I'm not sure I would be if I had to attend a board meeting right now. I'm not sure I wouldn't break down under the stress their conversation was sure to induce. Knowing they still had to deal with filling the open seats on the board and with the question of my contract renewal was bad enough. Having to sit and listen to the disagreements, I was sure would arise, was more than I could handle at the moment, even knowing I could do it wrapped in a cozy blanket with a bowl of ice cream in my hand.

It's understandable that after having Lilith's body fall at their feet last week, the board members would not be eager to return to the board room. In fact, I wouldn't be surprised if it were years before that closet was used again. Nor would it shock me if they picked a different room in which to hold their meetings from now on. For now, though, the choice to hold this particular meeting virtually was perfectly understandable. However, I was certain the tension and fear would still be palpable through the screens.

Interestingly, as much as the board members themselves were afraid to meet at the synagogue, none of them seemed to have any fear or hesitation about sending their younger children to Religious School over the course of this past week. I guess our messaging regarding the safety of the children was actually reassuring to most of the parents, or at least to those parents who were board members. ⅔ of our students showing up under the circumstances was remarkable! And we all appreciated the extra adult congregants who had offered to serve as guards (disguised as greeters) as well as the extra police patrols around the building.

What I found potentially perplexing was that all the parents appeared completely comfortable bringing students from Kitah Kochavim in for their individual lessons with me, despite the fact those tended to occur at times when there were few others in the building. But, what really blew my mind as I looked around was the fact that all of the students of Kitah Kochavim were present for class that evening. Of course, I did notice how their parents also stuck together as a group informally making a barrier between the students and the rest of the building.

I had expected the students to be a bit jumpy, but was surprised to see that not even Sam looked particularly anxious. I was afraid saying anything about this might open a can of worms, so I let the elephant in the corner of the room sleep. If they weren't afraid of the murderer coming after them or their parents, I was certainly not going to bring up the possibility! And hopefully the lesson I planned would further distract them from thoughts of the recent murders.

Since we had talked about what to do about finding a body between two towns, it made sense to me to talk about what to do with other things we find. I asked them to anonymously report whether they ever had something they lost returned to them and whether they had ever returned something to someone else. As I had hoped, that led to a conversation about how we might act differently when we know who the item belongs to or not. They shared stories of items found at their respective schools and summer camps, and what happened to these lost objects. While they talked, I quietly took notes so we could go over the similarities and differences they brought up.

After a robust conversation, without me even prompting them, the students asked if they could find a way to help return lost objects to their owners. I loved it and helped them to flesh out their ideas of how they might undertake this project. For the first time in what felt like decades (but was, in actuality, not even a month), I left the building feeling hopeful for the future.

Chapter 28
A Breath to Think

I got to experience my pride in my students a second time when I filled Rachel in on the latest news that evening once I got home after class.

"I'm glad your class went well, but what happened at the board meeting?" asked Rachel. "Did they renew your contract? People are starting to interview, you know."

My blood pressure rose at the reminder. "Don't remind me. I know. And I'm anxious enough as it is lately!"

"I know. I'm sorry. You know I'm asking out of love for you, right?"

"Of course I know you just want to make sure things end up working out OK for me, it's just..."

"So, they haven't put you out of this misery of uncertainty?"

"Yes and no," I hedged. "No one has said anything to me formally and I haven't seen anything in writing, so I don't know if I should be applying anywhere else."

"I'm so sorry, Shachar. This really sounds like torture."

"Well, they did have some other big issues to deal with, too," I commented. "I heard rumors they managed to agree on what to do about the vacant board positions, but no one is actually telling me what they agreed to. Are we having a nominating committee and congregational vote? Are they shifting people around so the executive committee is full and there are some empty spots on the general board? Are they leaving Leonard and Lilith's positions open until the annual vote in the spring? I have no idea."

"That sounds a bit unsettling. How will you know who you need to talk to for things to get done?"

"I'm sure they'll let Mina and me know at some point. In the meantime, I'll just keep doing what I'm doing."

"OK I don't know I'd be as calm as you, but more power to you."

"Thanks, but I'm not really calm. I'm actually overwhelmed and holding it all together with a bit of thread."

"Oh, honey! Haven't you at least heard rumors about your contract?"

"Rumors, sure, but like I said, nothing definite. Dani's been saying without Leonard and Lilith campaigning against me, tensions around here are sure to ease and she also thinks I'll get a good contract. But I also heard Elaine wondering whether people would decide not to renew my contract as a way of honoring Leonard and Lilith's memories. The third rumor going around is the one that sounds most plausible, though."

"Huh? You lost me. What's this third rumor? Are they giving you a new contract or not?"

"I've heard they'll be giving me a one-year extension, but only because they don't know how they could run a search until after the police have finished their investigation."

"That actually makes sense! So, what about this scenario has you worried?"

"A part of me thinks the reason rumor is going around is that someone thinks I'm guilty, or at least guilty enough, the police will tell me not to leave town."

"That's actually pretty thoughtful. They know you'd have to leave town to interview, so they're removing that obstacle."

"More like covering their own behinds. I get the impression someone is worried I'll sue if the reason I can't go to an interview, or something like that happens."

"I've gotta be honest, Shachar, that sounds super messed up."

"I know, but it's all just rumors right now. I've also heard they're supposedly going to be including a clause in this one year extension to make me take a forced Sabbatical."

"That doesn't sound bad to me! I'd love to take a sabbatical, but I'll have to wait another year and a half before I can do that."

"I won't lie. The opportunity to take a break sounds great. It's been really stressful and I could use some time to get recentered and re-energized. But it doesn't sound like they are granting me a sabbatical because they're trying to take care of me."

"Can't you pretend they are, even if that isn't their intent?"

"Maybe," I hesitated, "but I think it's because they don't want me here. I get the impression some people blame me for the murders. And those that don't, really don't like the fact I'm working with the police."

"What utter nonsense! Has anyone actually said either of those things to you?"

"No," I reluctantly admitted. "But..."

"No buts," Rachel jumped in. "You can't actually read people's minds, you know. Stop pretending you can!"

From there, our conversation quickly dissolved into debates about mind reading and other super powers. It felt really good to laugh with Rachel over something silly for a few minutes. And the invitation she offered right before we hung up, that I come spend part of my sabbatical with her, certainly made the whole thing seem much more appealing.

Chapter 29
A Suspect in Sight

"Does the fact you wanted to talk to me mean you have news?" I asked, hopeful Misha would tell me he caught the killer.

Not exactly news," he said as my hope plummeted, "but perhaps progress."

"Progress is good, right? I know you don't need more pressure to solve this, but if you did, it would make my life a lot easier."

"I'd love to be able to make your life easier," Misha said a bit shyly. "And I definitely want to catch this murderer. But, I don't have enough evidence to make an arrest stick right now."

"Not enough evidence? I thought you had both murder weapons."

"I do have both murder weapons, but I have nothing specific to link any of the suspects with them. Fingerprints on both are basically useless. There are too many people who have handled them. They both came from communal spaces in the synagogue, places where a lot of people had legitimate business, the Sanctuary and kitchen."

"Oh. I see how that could be a problem. But can't you tell which are the newest fingerprints? The top layer or something?"

"It's not that easy, unfortunately," Misha sounded slightly dejected. "I don't know all of the details of how it works, but our lab techs made it sound fairly impossible for us to identify the murderer by fingerprints on the weapons. Besides, too many people watch crime shows and know to use gloves so they don't leave prints in the first place."

I had to admit he had me there. I scrunched my brow. "You didn't want to talk to me just to tell me you're stuck, did you?" I groaned at the thought. "Attendance at services and basically all the other programs we offer except for Religious School classes has already dropped. And even when it comes to classes, absences are higher than usual even with added layers of protection the parents have helped put in place. People are scared. The board refused to meet in person. I'm worried people are going to start resigning their memberships." I rested my head on my hands. I really didn't know how much more of this I could take. It felt like my whole world was crumbling around me. I was watching the community I had spent so long growing and cultivating fall apart. I felt helpless. How could I be there for my congregants when I myself kept looking over my shoulder. Knowing there were job assassins out to get me was bad enough. The fear and distrust that came from a murderer on the loose was something else entirely.

"Hey," Misha said softly. "It's going to be OK, Shachar. Really. My team and I have solved lots of murders. And communities have a way of healing, even after something traumatic as what you're dealing with here."

I desperately wanted to believe him. So I rubbed my eyes and sat up straighter. "OK. So you need evidence. And you think I can help with that?"

"Yes! At least, I hope so."

"Does that also mean you have a suspect in mind?"

"I have a psych profile. Those aren't conclusive evidence, but sometimes they help. It seems our murderer thought Leonard was dumb, or soft in the head, and Lilith was a backstabber."

"That could be practically anyone!" I exclaimed, failing to keep the despair and frustration out of my voice.

"Maybe," he agreed, "but the list you made explaining some of the connections between the victims and the most likely pool of suspects was quite helpful with narrowing things down."

"I'm glad I was able to do something to help," I shrugged as the corners of my mouth turned up ever so slightly. "Is there maybe something else I could do?"

"Actually, that's why I wanted to talk to you."

"Oh?"

"So, we couldn't use the murder weapons to find fingerprints, but we did find something else odd when we examined them in our lab."

The suspense was almost killing me.

"Both weapons had a single hair somewhere on them. And the hairs matched. But, before you get super excited about that, we couldn't do a DNA test on either hair."

"So, are you saying the hairs are evidence the two murders are linked? Or that they're another dead end."

"The first. But that's not even the best part. Both hairs had something on them one of the techs identified as bike grease."

"Bike grease!?! What?"

"That's what I was hoping you could tell me. I know we both think some of the suspects have already been eliminated, but for the sake of this question, let's assume no one has been completely cleared, OK?"

"OK," I agreed, still quite puzzled.

"Is there anyone on this list of suspects who doesn't just occasionally ride a bike but who is a bit more serious about it? Someone who might repair their own slipped chain or a problem that involves grease?"

I gave the question some serious thought. "I'm not positive, but I think I've seen Abner Kleinman biking around. And Emma Silverman sometimes rides her bike to her Bat Mitzvah lessons. But she's never liked to get messy either playing outside or when doing an art project, so she probably doesn't fix her own bike. The only one I know for sure is a serious biker is Dani..." my voice trailed off.

"Dani? Interesting," Misha said enigmatically.

"But Dani is always so nice and so supportive!" I exclaimed. "You can't possibly think...."

"What I think is that the physical evidence we have has only been enough to give us questions. Lilith's death was an opportunity to find more clues and evidence, but it also threw a big wrench and complication into what I had been thinking when we were just looking for Leonard's murderer." He let out a small sigh. "I don't think I can solve this one based on evidence and alibis alone."

"What else is there? You're not saying you're giving up, are you?" a bit of panic crept into my voice.

"No, I'm not giving up. If I didn't have someone involved I considered an ally, my next step would be re-questioning everyone and being a bit more forceful about it. But...." he trailed off thoughtfully. "Maybe this is something you'd be willing to do with me?"

I didn't have to hear anything more to know I would agree to whatever he asked if it would bring us closer to a resolution.

Chapter 30
Operation Confession

A while later, I really wasn't sure why I agreed to help do this. Rachel thought it was because I found Misha dreamy. I told her she was being ridiculous. But I did enjoy our conversations. I wouldn't let my trepidation stop this killer from getting caught.

A female police officer whose name I didn't know looked me over one more time. "Looks good," she said, "nothing's visible. Now it's time to test the sound."

"OK. How do I do that?" I asked, hoping it didn't involve anything too tricky.

"Transmission should already be on from you to the team. But, you'll have to turn on that little earpiece if you want to be able to hear them too."

It sounded easy enough. I turned on the small device and fit it into my ear. "Hi, team," I said, not knowing who exactly was on the other end listening.

I was reassured to hear Misha's voice replying, "we hear you, Shachar. Could you get the officer with you to say something so we can make sure we're picking up more than just your voice?"

"OK," I replied, then looked at the woman across from me.

Her lips quirked up and she said, "you don't need to talk down into your shirt. They should be able to hear you just fine."

I heard chuckling in my ear.

"Besides," she continued, "you want to be natural. Otherwise the suspect will realize something is going on."

"That does make sense," I conceded.

"And we can hear both of you just fine," said Misha's voice in my ear. "Remember, we're here with you, and we can step in to help the moment you need us."

"Right. That's what you said before. But how will you know I need help?"

"We're going to pick a code word right now. Something you aren't likely to say randomly as part of this conversation, but isn't so strange it sends warning bells to the suspect, leading to them fleeing and us getting involved in a big chase."

"OK...." I trailed off as I thought for a minute. "What about 'chocolate'?"

"'Chocolate' it is," said the voice in my ear. "I have faith in you. If we have the right person, you'll get our suspect to confess to murder or reveal something only the killer would know. If our theory regarding motive is true, the suspect will want you to know these murders were done intending to protect you."

I still had major butterflies in my stomach, but reminded myself no one thought I was in any danger. I'd spent plenty of time alone with this person before, and nothing bad had happened. In fact, I might even be the safest person around if the murderer really was killing people who were perceived as threats to me in some way.

Dani and I met up in the parking lot at the start of one of the beautiful nature trails in the area and greeted each other.

"Thanks for agreeing to a walk," I said. "I needed to get out of the building."

"How are you doing?" she asked. "A lot's been going on at the synagogue."

"That's an understatement," I said while trying not to let the snort escape. "First all of the stress over contract renewal or not and now two dead bodies. Most of the time,

I'm not sure what to think right now," I admitted, trying to figure out how I was going to extract anything resembling a confession. "I mean, you know I was having some differences of opinion with Lilith...." I trailed off.

"I know. I tried to warn you she could be a bit of a backstabber."

Was this my opening? "I don't know," I hedged. "I do think she had my back for a while. If she never did, then she did a really good job pulling the wool over my eyes. She genuinely seemed to care about me and love my ideas when I first got here."

"When your ideas matched hers?"

"I suppose."

"But as soon as you were no longer her little puppet but started sharing your own brilliant and much-needed ideas with the community, there was a strain on your relationship with her, right?"

"Sure. I felt more frustrated in general, but still thought things were fine...."

"When she started to say mean things behind your back, they were pretty subtle, but that's when I first told you to watch out for her. Now aren't you relieved she's not holding you back any more? You can do all those amazing things you have been dreaming about to enact some positive changes in this community.”

“Relieved!?!? Why would I be relieved someone I know is not just dead but was deliberately murdered?!?”

“Because she can’t hurt you any more now.”

“What do you mean she can’t hurt me anymore? Now it’s worse, because there’s a fairly good chance the police think I had something to do with killing her!” I said as I put a bit of panic into my voice.

“Why would they think that? You are the best person I know, kind, moral, caring.”

“Thank you. That’s sweet of you to say. But the way I see it, even though both Leonard and Lilith had potential enemies, only a few people actually had issues with both of them recently. And, as you know, I’m one of those few people.”

“Sure, but I know you didn’t hurt them. And now that Leonard and Lilith are gone, your contract will get renewed and you’ll be able to stay with me, with us!”

“What do you mean?”

“You must know! They were the ones really working against you! And you were so stressed and anxious because of them. Now you can do the amazing work you do without anyone stopping you!"

"What if they weren't the only ones?"

"Then those others better watch out."

"What?!?"

"Someone clearly has your back. They don't want to see an idiot push you away because they can't see your brilliance."

"You mean Leonard?"

"Yes, I mean Leonard. He always had mush for brains. Dumb as a candlestick."

Did this count as a confession or inside knowledge? Or was it just a spewing of figures of speech. I must have stood there with my mouth hanging open for just a beat too long because suddenly I heard a voice in my ear say, "suggestive, but not enough for a conviction...."

"Um," I swallowed. "Are you talking about what his dead body looked like? I thought no one else had seen him. Or not more than his shoes and part of his legs."

"Well, when someone is hit in the head with enough force, you can see what little they had for brains."

"Where did you hear Leonard was hit on the head?" I tried to sound casual, not judgmental or anxious.

"I don't know. I thought everyone knew. I'm sure I heard a bunch of people say it."

"But, if he was hit on the head, how did so much of his body get under the reader's table?" I tried to ask in a neutrally inquisitive tone. "He must have been dragged by his shirt or something."

"Bingo!" I heard in my ear. "Can you get her to say more about the shirt?"

I wondered what it was about the shirt that excited the team so much. Had they gotten fingerprints or other evidence off of it? I wasn't sure where to go with this, so I tried asking, "wouldn't that have ripped his shirt?"

"No, it was a strong shirt. Rayon herringbone shirts don't tear. They're very durable."

"How do you know his shirt was made of rayon herringbone?" I asked nervously.

"That's the type he wore a lot."

"Really? I don't think I'd ever seen him in a shirt like that before...."

"Maybe you just didn't realize."

"Maybe," I shrugged and glanced at my watch. "Oh no, I need to head back for this afternoon's Bar Mitzvah lesson," I said.

"Thanks for walking with me. This was an...interesting conversation."

Less than thirty minutes later, I was once again surrounded by police officers.

"I'm sorry I didn't get a confession for you," I said with my head hanging down into my hands.

"No apology required," said Misha.

"You may not have gotten a confession, but you did uncover some really great leads," said one of the other members of the team.

"I did?" I brightened up a little at that thought. "You mean the stuff about Leonard's shirt? That was really weird."

"Here are the lab and search results," said the female officer who had helped put on my wire. She handed the envelope to Misha.

His eyes rapidly scanned the document, then he leapt out of his seat with a cry of triumph. "The shirt Leonard was found in was rayon herringbone. And...." he paused for dramatic effect "he did not own any other shirts like it!"

"I don't suppose we were lucky enough to get a fingerprint or trace evidence off of the shirt?" asked the team member who had spoken before.

"Not yet, but the lab is also going over the clothes Lilith was wearing. Between the two, there's a good chance we'll find the crucial evidence we need to make this conviction stick. In the meantime, I say we have plenty to bring our suspect in, ask some more questions, and keep her in a cell at least temporarily," said Misha with some satisfaction in his voice.

He offered to walk me out, and I gratefully accepted. I hadn't realized how shaky I had become until I stood and tried to walk on my own. Misha smiled at me understandingly without saying a word. After a few deep breaths, I felt a lot steadier, and was even able to ask if he might be able to come talk to Kitah Kochavim and probably their parents and the board members to tell them who the murderer once the arrest was made and to reassure them all of their safety.

Thankfully, he agreed readily, and I hoped it would not be long before he could fulfill that promise.

Chapter 31
Denouement

It felt a bit surreal to once again be gathered in the Chapel with the students in Kitah Kochavim, their parents, some board members, Mina, and Detective Tara. Unlike the last time this particular group of people was assembled in this spot, the atmosphere was more hopeful and much less anxious and apprehensive. Even though he hadn't said so, in Detective Tara's "mandatory invitation," there was the assumption there must have been a big break in the case(s). He and his team had already had multiple conversations with just about everyone in the room. So, at least a few of us were expecting a bit of a "Hercule Poirot Moment" where we would hear details of how these murders were committed, the clues the killer inadvertently left behind, and, perhaps most importantly, the identity of the killer.

I suspected I knew the answer to that last bit of information. It wasn't just because of the conversations Misha and I'd had throughout his investigation. I also noticed there was one person who had been present at the service led by Kitah Kochavim who was not sitting with the rest of us now. Well, two if you count the stranger, but I had really become convinced these murders were "an inside job." After all, the stranger hadn't been here when Lilith was killed. And a stranger had, we all hoped, no way of getting into the building undetected.

Whatever small part I might have played in helping identify the murderer, I was happy to let Misha be the one to take center stage at this gathering. He cleared his throat and began speaking, "first I want to thank Rabbi Whyte for graciously ceding her time with these incredible students so I could talk with all of you together."

I nodded in acknowledgement, but didn't say anything.

"My gratitude toward Rabbi Whyte extends not just to her time tonight, but also for her help throughout this investigation. And the same can be said of each and every one of you."

"So, did you catch the killer or not?" blurted out Ethan. I barely held back a giggle.

You can always trust kids, and even some teens, to blurt out exactly what they are thinking. Clearly, by the low rumble spreading around the room, Ethan wasn't the only one who wanted to know.

"Yes, I believe we have found the killer and rest assured that person will be held accountable for the lives of both Leonard Steinberg and Lilith Polshani." Sighs of relief greeted this announcement. "And furthermore, we have no reason to believe any of the rest of you are in any danger now."

"How can you be so sure of that?" asked Sherry Kahn. "Two of the board members were killed! Are the rest of us really not in danger anymore?"

"Correct," said Detective Tara succinctly before continuing, "let me take you through what happened."

"OK." said nearly everyone in a chorus.

"First, some background," he began while another officer wrote things down on a giant post-it for those who are visual learners. "There were a couple of really big things, and a few smaller ones, you all told me were happening in your community at the time Leonard was murdered." He held up fingers as he enumerated. "Mina told us Rabbi Whyte received a scary, antisemitic phone call a few days before Leonard's body was found. Between the caterers and people coming for your class service, there were people in the building not everyone knew. With the rise in antisemitism all over the country, the idea Leonard was killed in an act of antisemitic violence was a possibility."

"But, what about all of our security measures?" asked Abner Kleinman. "How could a murderer have gotten in unnoticed?"

"There are ways, and I have been talking to the head of your security committee about what upgrades could be made. But, we always ranked the possibility of Leonard having been killed by a stranger as a low one, even once we learned the caller referred to Leonard in particular. The theory of the antisemitic killer was put to rest when Lilith was found dead, too. It didn't seem likely a murderous, antisemitic psychopath was somehow getting into the synagogue building and picking people off one at a time. That's very out of character and doesn't fit any psychological profile for a hate-based serial killing."

"So, you're saying it's not my fault?" asked Mina. "That whoever this killer is, there was no reason for me to have denied that person entrance?"

"Exactly," he reassured her as she sighed and deflated like a balloon as her guilt leaked away.

"There had been a really big, loud fight at the board meeting a couple nights before our service," said Emma. "It scared all of us. Were these people killed because of something that happened at a meeting?!?!" The idea seemed preposterous to her.

"Unfortunately, almost any time people get together and end up getting really super mad at each other, there's a possibility of violence if no one can get the people who are fighting to calm down," chimed in Avital Rosenberg.

"When I talked to you, at first no one who mentioned this loud fight actually knew what it was about. Some of you thought it had to do with Sam's upcoming Bar Mitzvah, to which I hope you'll invite me," he said, winking at the kid. "Others thought it was either about the boiler or about whether or not to renew Rabbi Whyte's contract."

"But, whatever the fight at the board meeting was about isn't really what was important. What mattered more was what the murderer thought it was about," he paused to let that sink in. "And my team and I needed to figure out who might want both Leonard and Lilith dead. A lot of people were having trouble with one or the other of them, but only a handful of folk would benefit from both of their deaths."

I noticed that Emma and Hannah were clinging to each other and a lot of other people were shifting in their seats or looking around the room at each other. Was Detective Tara drawing this out on purpose? Was he trying to torture everyone?

"To make a long story short," he continued, "my team and I first thought Rabbi Whyte," he turned to me and gave a sheepish shrug, "would benefit from both Leonard and Lilith being out of the picture. But," he held up a hand before the clamor could start, "we had already ruled her out as a suspect both because of her strong moral fiber and because she didn't have the opportunity. Her movements were all accounted for. We know how fond of her many of you are, but we think Rabbi Whyte only has one superfan here. A superfan goes beyond admiring a person to wanting to take care of things and, in their minds, make things easier for the person they adore."

The kids looked at each other and shouted, "that lady who substituted! What's her name? She seemed like she was trying to do everything just like Rabbi Whyte!"

"She even cut her hair and started wearing different clothes," piped up Emma.

There was a chorus of agreement among the students and looks of bewildered shock on the faces of the adults in the room. It was clear the kids had noticed something important the board members had not.

"The lady who substituted," Mina repeated under her breath. "Dani??!? Dani Chaco?!? You're saying it was Dani who killed them both?" asked Mina with wide eyes.

"Yes," Misha confirmed. "There were a few crucial clues that led us to her, including some bike grease left in some very compromising locations."

"I wondered why she isn't here with the rest of us," marveled Avital. "I never would have guessed. Dani, a murderer?"

"She thought she was protecting Rabbi Whyte, here," said Detective Tara. "But none of you need to worry about her hurting anyone else in this community for a long, long time. We arrested her earlier today, and while I can't predict what a jury will say or do, I will say we have a very strong case against her."

I stood up, "And I am grateful the board has granted me some time off to process all of this, but I promise I won't disappear until after your Bar Mitzvah, Sam. And I'll be back before yours, Emma," I said. "As the joke goes, they tried to kill us, we won, let's eat. There are some treats in the other room so none of you faint on your way home tonight."

Epilogue

Following my friend Rabbi Rachel Rubin's advice, I thanked Misha by giving him a bag of dried apricots. I had to explain the joke: In Hebrew, they're called Mishmish. He liked that. And he now knows a lot of other Hebrew words and Jewish customs, too. He's not sure yet whether he will convert, but he says he's enjoying learning about Judaism, and I'm enjoying teaching him.

Sam did a great job at his Bar Mitzvah, as I knew he would. He did have me check the Bima before he would come join me up front, just in case there was another body on the Bima, not that any of us really thought there would be. Better safe than sorry, though, so I didn't mind checking for him. Best of all, he had gotten over the fear that he, himself, would drop dead in the middle of the service. I'll take my small victories where I can get them.

Now, I look forward to relaxing and processing all the craziness that's happened with a long visit with my best friend.

I'm even looking forward to the teasing about Misha.

www.ingramcontent.com/pod-product-compliance
Lightning Source LLC
Chambersburg PA
CBHW071130180726
48291CB00007B/2117